Wild Boy
The First Shirt

Peter Ransley has written extensively for television. His BBC adaptation of Sarah Waters' "Fingersmith" was a BAFTA nomination for Best Series. His book, "The Hawk" was filmed starring Helen Mirren. Among his various awards, Peter received the Royal Television Society's Writer's Award for the BBC's Play for Today with "Minor Complications", which launched the charity AvMA, promoting safety and justice for people suffering from medical accidents.

Peter's novels include the *Tom Neave* trilogy, set in the time of the English Civil War: "Plague Child", "Cromwell's Blessing" and "The King's List".

More can be discovered at www.peterransley.co.uk

Also by Peter Ransley

The Tom Neave trilogy
Plague Child
Cromwell's Blessing
The King's List

The Hawk
The Price
Bright Hair About the Bone

Wild Boy

The First Shirt

Peter Ransley

Grosvenor House
Publishing Limited

This book is published by
Grosvenor House Publishing Ltd
Link House
140 The Broadway, Tolworth, Surrey, KT6 7HT.
www.grosvenorhousepublishing.co.uk

This book is a work of fiction. Any resemblance to
people or events, past or present, is purely coincidental.

A CIP record for this book
is available from the British Library

ISBN 978-1-83975-152-3

This book is dedicated to my grandchildren,
Finlay, whose writing gave me the idea, Blake,
Nina and Sigrid.

Fourways is a fictional London tower block within sight of Grenfell Tower, the subject of an inquiry which killed 78 people in the fire of 2017. Desmond's friend Tom, referred to as killed there and his mother are both fictional characters.

People call me Des

Sometimes they call me other things, particularly Almost. I call him Almost because he is Almost, but not my dad. I am eight and three-quarters. I can write but I cannot add up very well. That's what Miss Hancock, my teacher says.

The Dilemma

Every story has a Dilemma, Miss Hancock says. A Dilemma, a Climax and a Conclusion, or it is not a proper story. My Dilemma is that Chips keeps going wrong. Chips is Almost's motorbike. He works for To-Your-Door, delivering curries and fish and chips. I call it Chips because sometimes, when Almost is in a good mood, he lets me have a bag of chips.

The night it happened it was raining. It wasn't really, but always start a story with rain, Miss Hancock says. The more the better. So it was pouring down when Almost was out with Chips. The rest is true. Almost.

We live in a flat, four floors up in Fourways Tower. I was in bed but could not sleep because of my cough. Almost was off on his evening delivery. I heard him trying to start Chips. There was a big bang. From our window I saw Mum run out.

Almost was hitting the bike with a spanner. It went clang clang clang bang bang bang, poor Chips. Mum tried to stop Almost and he shoved her and she almost fell over, poor mum. Then Almost drew his foot back and gave Chips the biggest kick ever. It hurt him more than Chips. He hopped and he yelled and the window below us opened and Mrs Griffin, whom we called Mrs Grumble, shouted at him. I dribbled water down on her and mum was cross but Almost laughed and said it was rain wasn't it Des?

Almost couldn't work without Chips. So we went on benefits and Mum took me to school for breakfast. I hate it. Not just because it is porridge but because of Stewart and Henry. They are horrible. Their mums bring them in BMWs. It's not what they say, it's what they do. They look at me and grin at one another.

"Mmmmmm!" Stewart rubbed his stomach. "I had bacon and egg".

"Mmmmmm!" Henry licked his lips. "Sausages and mushrooms. "

I went for them. Like Almost went for Chips. I went for them until Miss Hancock pulled me off.

"What did you do that for? " Mum said. "Please don't fight any more or they'll put you in isolation."

"What's isolation?" I said.

"Locked up. Like ..."

"Like what?"

She shook her head and didn't say any more.

After porridge next day at school I had an apple. That was all right and I sneaked a number of apples into my school bag for Mum. She likes apples.

I was wearing a crap pair of trainers from the charity shop. Henry was wearing a new pair of Nikes with flash red stripes. He asked me what sort of trainers mine were, serious-like and Stewart said he would like a pair like that and they both laughed. I remembered what my mum said and said nothing but Henry trod on my lace which was undone and I slipped and crashed into a desk and half the apples fell out of my bag. I went to hit Henry but Miss Hancock came in. You wait, I said, you wait!

The lesson was about stories. I like stories. I like them cos you become someone else and live a different life. I like living a different life.

Miss Hancock said don't forget every story has a dilemma, a climax and a conclusion. It could be about a football game, a rabbit - anything, so long as it has those things. At the end of the lesson I had forgotten about bashing them but they hadn't. Henry was saying something to Miss Hancock who told me to stay behind and opened my bag and took out all the apples. She said I musn't take more apples than I need at breakfast. You can't eat all those apples, can you, Des, she said. They're not for me I said. They're for my mum. She likes fruit.

Oh, Des, she said. Oh. That was all for a bit. Oh Des. She got out her handkerchief, blew her nose and looked out of the window. I thought she was cross with me again but she gave me an apple, the biggest and the reddest of them all and said it was all right to take one for your Mum and I was not to forget to write my story for the next day.

I don't understand grown-ups. Sometimes something is wrong, then the same thing is right. I gave my Mum the big red apple and she started crying. See what I mean?

Then I wanted to watch a story on the telly but Mum said I had to write my own story first for Miss Hancock. I yelled at her I didn't *know* no stories about rabbits or football like Henry and Stewart! They wore football shirts and went to the match! She still wouldn't let me watch telly and she wouldn't hold me or kiss me until I wrote my story.

I was so miserable and stared out of the window. I thought of what Miss Hancock said. Every story starts with rain. I wrote on ruled paper in my best handwriting. *It was raining.* Then I did not know what to say and stared out of the window. Then I wrote *a lot.* I did not know what to say again so I looked out of the other window. There was poor old Chips. So I wrote the story you see here. *People call me Des* then fell asleep with my pencil in my hand.

In the morning it was raining like my story and Almost was still asleep but Mum kissed me and said my writing was good. I could see she had been crying and I knew it was something to do with Almost so I hugged my Mum. There were pools in the playground and my trainers were wet. I hate my trainers but I didn't say anything cos I know it upsets Mum.

Miss Hancock read out Henry's story about the football match but she never read out mine. At the end of class she called me over. I thought here we go again. She said my writing had a very good Dilemma and an even better Climax but there was no Conclusion. I said that's because there isn't one. Every story must have a Conclusion, Desmond, she said. Mine hasn't, I said.

Whatever I do is wrong. When school was over Miss Hancock showed my story to Stewart's dad, Mike. He laughed just like Stewart and Henry did at my trainers and things. I would have punched him one but he is bigger than me and Mum was there. I ran to her and said I never ever wanted to go to school again. She held me and said Miss Hancock wanted to talk to me but I never wanted to see her again either.

Then Stewart's dad said my story was very good. Stewart was very good at lego he said but he couldn't write a story like that. That's because I don't have no lego I said and he didn't know what to say. Any road, I said, Miss Hancock says my story is not finished because it has no Conclusion. He knelt down. He has a bit of a beard and a smile. That's what we want to talk about, Des, he said. I didn't know what to say. When people look at you like that, they're either going to be very nice or more nasty than ever.

Mike's going to give us a lift home, Mum said. When we got to the BMW I heard Stewart say to his dad I don't want him in our car. Why not, his dad said. Because his trainers stink, Stewart said. Get in! his dad shouted, real angry. I got in the back with my Mum. It smelt clean and it started right away unlike Chips and was really really quiet. He stopped near poor old Chips and opened his boot. It was like a treasure chest in there, batteries and chisels and wires and things. Mike owns a garage, Mum said.

Mike tried to start Chips and it made a horrible screeching noise. He shook his head and took a bit of the engine to bits. I saw Almost's face at the window. I thought hello. Here's trouble. Almost was down in a flash, hair sticking out, fists clenched.

What do you think you're doing he said. Trying to start your motorbike Mike said. Almost told him to sod off. I thought Mike was going to chuck his chisel at him but he threw it in the boot with the rest of his stuff. Mum tried to talk to Almost but he told her to shut it, he was going to fix it himself when he got the stuff and I thought that was that.

CONCLUSION

Mike said to Almost had he read the story? What story? Almost said and Mum gave him my story. Here we go, I thought. Almost never reads that much. He ran his finger along the lines He muttered. Then he sniffed. Then he laughed. He shoved it back at mum and muttered to Mike he couldn't afford to pay him.

Just pay me for the parts, Mike said. When you can. Almost turned away and Mike screwed and unscrewed and tried to start it. It went off then died. Then Almost held things for him and after a bit it went thrum thrum thrum and everybody cheered and Almost went back to deliver food and everything was all right. For a bit. The end. Author Desmond Taylor.

A Proper Dad

I asked Mum why everyone had a Dad except me. You have Almost, she said. I mean a proper Dad, I said. Like Stewart's Dad, Mike.

"With a BMW?" she said.

"No. Just like Mike."

"We didn't get on."

"You don't get on with Almost."

She laughed and shook her head. "We do most of the time, but things are well ... a bit difficult at the moment. They were even more difficult with your father and he wouldn't want to see you."

"Why?"

She hugged me, laughed more and at the same time her eyes were wet. She said he didn't want kids. It was one of the reasons why they broke up. He wouldn't want to see you even if she knew where he was, which she didn't.

I began to wonder what my dad was like? Where he was? Why didn't I have a dad like Stewart's, who bought him things? Stewart kept on telling people how he was building the biggest crib in lego for baby Jesus until I was fed up of him and baby Jesus. When Miss Hancock told us there were various religions with different Gods I asked her which was the biggest. She said there was no biggest. They all had different beliefs.

Why do you ask? When I told her I wanted to ask him for a big lego set she said you're supposed to ask God for things for other people. What's the use of that? I said. They've all got legos except me.

I prayed for a bigger lego set than Stewart's and nothing happened and when I told Mum she said it wasn't Christmas yet. She had a red eye almost closed and said she'd had a fall but I knew it was Almost giving her one.

I wondered if we would get more things if we went to church and asked why we didn't go. Almost said it was because we were bad and Mum said it was because she didn't believe in God.

Stewart told me God lived in the church he went to. When Mike, Stewart's dad, said he would take me I asked if I could go and see him but really I wanted to see Stewart's Lego. Mike took me.

It was terrific. The Lego, not the church. The church was horrible, cold and doomy, but I wanted the Lego as soon as I saw it. There were two reindeers and a big star and a baby. The Vicar was a funny man wearing woman's clothes and a white collar but he told good stories. He said there was a God who sent baby Jesus to save us. He waved something burning which sent a funny, magic smell in the air. Afterwards, people put money in his box. Mike put a whole blue five pound note in. I said if I brought my box round would people put money in it and everybody laughed. Why are people always laughing at me?

They talked boring and I thought if God is so boring I don't want to meet him. I crept to the back of the church to the Lego. I was frightened and wanted to run but at the same time I couldn't. Hello? I whispered. Is anyone there? There were funny echoes. I felt someone was whispering but didn't know what he was saying. It was almost dark but there was a queer light over the Lego. I meant to take the star or the reindeer but found myself taking the crib. They won't miss a crib, I thought, stuffing it up my jumper. But that crafty sod Stewart was watching me and jumped at me. I fell on the stone floor and cut my head.

Mike was cross with me and phoned Mum to get me while the vicar bandaged my head. The crib had broken up. The vicar said he didn't do lego - could I help him put it together again?

He asked me why I took it and I said because I didn't have no lego. I wanted the star really but I took the baby.

"Why the baby?" the vicar asked.

"For mum," I said.

"Why mum?"

"So she could ask him," I said.

"Ask him. Ask him what, Des?"

"If he could stop Almost bashing her."

"Who's Almost?" he said.

He's almost my dad and he's not I mumbled. Sometimes he's all right. He's good at football. He used to be a goalie but he wanted to be a striker.

The vicar tucked his skirt round his legs and asked me to help him put baby Jesus together again so that other people could ask him questions. "Does he answer them?" I asked and he laughed. He had a way of laughing which made his whole belly shake.

"I hope he does answer them," he said. "Sometimes I feel he does." He scratched his head which was just beginning to go grey. "Sometimes I feel he doesn't."

"What's the good of that?" I said.

He laughed until I thought his whole belly was going to fall off. "I ask myself that every single day," he said, wiping his eyes with a corner of his skirt. "Every day of my life, Des, it is Des isn't it?" By this time I was laughing as well, you couldn't help laughing with him and his big belly.

The door banged, going boom boom boom round the whole church. It was Mum. She ran down the tiles her heels going angry click clack click clack on the tiles. That's me finished I thought. Her face was creased-over-cross until she saw my bandaged head and she held me and I burst out crying and she said to the vicar what is it I'd better take him to the hospital which made me cry even more.

"Don't worry," he said. "He's all right." He told her he used to be a nurse.

She asked him why he left and he gave her one of his funny smiles. "Give up something useful?"

"Yes." She looked at the floor, sniffed and blew her nose.

"I ask myself that every day," he said. He looked at her red eye which was almost closed now. "That's a nasty eye," he said. "How did you do that?"

"I fell," she said. People are funny. They say nothing but they say a lot. He made a sort of face and she said has Des been telling you fairy tales? You don't want to listen to him.

He gave her one of his smiles. "He has a way with words," he said.

"You can say that again," she said, grabbing my arm so tight it hurt. "You ought to be ashamed of yourself."

I pulled away from her. "You said you didn't believe in God!"

"Never mind that!" she said, going beetroot red. "Stealing from a church!"

"Just a minute," the vicar said. "Let me see that eye."

There was something in his voice again. He took mum into a light and lifted her chin. He got her eye open with his finger and thumb and shone the light in it. She pulled away sharp.

"Did that hurt?"

"A bit."

"You should go to A and E," he said. "Now".

He rang them and when they said how long it would take he said to mum do you have a car? You're joking she said and so he took us and she phoned Almost on the way. As soon as they saw her in hospital they took her away. She had not come back when Almost came in. I didn't want to see him because he had bashed mum and I didn't want him bashing me but he was all nice when he saw the Vicar and did a sort of funny dance with his fingers and muttered something.

The Vicar said are you a Catholic? Was he said. Was. Committed enough sins to be one since, he said, and laughed. The vicar laughed but neither of them was laughing really and the vicar had to go back to the church and see if God had arrived yet.

A doctor came and said mum was sleeping. There had been a lot of blood inside the eye and an infection and he had given her antibiotics and how did it happen? She tripped over a rug and banged her eye on the arm of a chair Almost said. The doctor looked at me. For a moment I was going to say there isn't a rug in our flat. But I saw Almost looking at me and said nothing.

Mum was funny. Woozy. One eye bandaged. Propped up in bed. Almost cried. Suddenly cried. He couldn't stop. I had never seen him cry before. The two of them seemed to stop seeing me. It was as if I wasn't there. Almost said it wouldn't happen again. You've said that before she said. Why don't you get a proper job? Mike the garage owner will help you. I will, I will he said. You've said that before, too, she said.

I didn't want to go home with Almost for I was afraid he would bash me but I had to. I rode on the back of Chips. It was all right until it began pissing down and I got soaked. I feared he would get drunk when we got back and I remembered what mum did once. Because I was wet he gave me the keys while he was covering up his bike and I ran up to the flat before him. There was a bottle of wine in the fridge almost full. I poured it down the sink. There was a bit of gin. I poured that down too and dropped the bottles in the bin just as he came in.

"It's a good job you like pizzas," he said.

"I don't like tomato and mozzy ones," I said.

"Well it's what there is. Eat it." He cut up a piece and shoved it at my mouth. I shut it tight. He tried to shove it in and I spat it out. I thought he was going to clout me one but he said suit yourself and shoved a piece in his mouth and then another and another.

"Are there any sausages?" I said.

"You and your bloody sausages! Eat your pizza! There's nothing else".

"I want my Mum."

He banged his fist on the table so my plate of pizza fell on the floor. "Now there's no pizza and no Mum," he shouted.

I began to cry. I was afraid to cry but I could feel the tears creeping down my cheeks as he jumped up and opened the fridge.

"I'm sure there was a bottle there," he muttered. He looked in the room near the telly and in the cupboard where the gin was. He opened the fridge again and slammed it shut. Then he saw the bottles in the bin.

"I can't believe she drank all that," he said.

"Maybe that's why she fell," I said.

I didn't mean to say that. The words just seemed to come out of my mouth.

"What did you say?" he said. He gripped the wine bottle. "What did you say?"

I was frightened but I stood there unable to move as he came towards me. The door bell rang. He stopped. I don't think he would have answered it but it rang again. Long. Very long.

"Who's there," he shouted.

"The vicar," the voice said over the door phone. "Come to see if you're ok." I never thought Almost was going to press the door bell but he did.

The vicar was soaked like me. His wet hair stuck to his head and a drop of water hung on the end of his nose. He looked at the splashed pizza on the floor and the broken plate. They both looked at it and there seemed nothing else in the flat and neither looked as if he was going to say anything so I had to say something.

"Was God there?" I said.

"God?" the vicar said.

"In the church when you got back."

They both smiled, but they were proper smiles. You could tell. "God," the vicar said. "God. Yes, I think God was around a bit today." Almost asked him if he would like a cup of coffee and the vicar said a hot cup of coffee would be very nice, thank you.

As the vicar was leaving Almost asked if mum would be all right and the vicar said: "Oh yes. Yes, they caught it in time."

"Thank God," Almost said. "Thank God".

My eyes were closing but when I got into bed I couldn't sleep for thinking about Mum. She always read me a story and there was no story. I couldn't sleep without a story. I got up. The flat was very quiet and full of shadows. It was so quiet I thought Almost had gone out for a drink and I was frightened of what he would be like when he got back. There was a click click click. Then a funny snap snap snap. I hid behind a chair then crept towards the noise in Mum and Almost's bedroom. Almost had opened an old suitcase of his. He had taken a book from it. He never read books. He put his finger in the book to follow a line. "Men do not" ... he said. "Men do not hide a ... hide a - " He saw me and shouted at me to get back to bed. I ran back pulling the duvet over my head shaking as I heard him come in. I pretended to be asleep. He pulled back the duvet.

"I know you're not asleep," he said. He shook me. "Des. Des. What's this?" He shook me. He was holding the book he had taken from the case, pointing to a word. "What's this word?" It was a very old book and the words were difficult.

"C - candle," I said.

"That's right," he said. "Men - do -not-light-a -

"Candle," I said.

"- and, and - hide-it-under-a - a - "

"Stone."

"Stone - but put - it in a - in a - Candlestick!" he shouted.

So we read the story together which he told me his grandma used to read to him as a boy and so I fell asleep.

Miss Hancock said she liked my story and asked after class if it was true. You can make up stories to be what you want them to be, can't you? I said. Er, yes, she said, yes, certainly. Does Almost have a Bible? Yes, I said. He said the Bible is true. Is it?

She took off her funny spectacles and then she put them on again. "Yes," she said. "Yes. Well." She hummed and hawed. "Well, the people who wrote the Bible wrote it down. Just like you, Des."

Inspector Grandad

Half-term holidays. Who invented them? Mum says. She used to leave me with Almost while she did odd cleaning jobs but now he's working at Mike's garage she has to take me everywhere. First call was Grandad,

I jumped up and down in excitement. "Can he take me to Spacemen? At the science museum?"

"No. He's not well," she said.

"But he promised!"

"You don't want to listen to him."

"He said he would!" I couldn't help crying, I couldn't because adults say one thing and mean another.

In Grandad's small drive was his old car. It was all rust and dirt except for the shiny new tyre Almost had fitted. "Be nice to him," she said, as she put a key in the lock. "He used to be a policeman. An Inspector."

"Inspector Grandad! Did he arrest people?"

"Yes. He'll arrest you if you don't behave yourself. But ever since Grandma died he's not been very well."

The place smelt of pooh. He was asleep, scrunched up in his chair with his hair in grey wisps rising and falling. There were dirty dishes on the floor and piled up in the sink. Mum closed her eyes for a minute and then began washing up. The noise woke him

"What happened to the cleaner?" she said.

"What?"

"What happened to the cleaner!" she shouted.

"Don't shout he said. I've found my hearing aids. One of them. The cleaner hasn't arrived."

"I can see that."

"You have to be nice to her or she won't come at all," he said. "Hello Des. How are you, old friend?"

I folded my arms, stuck my lips out and said nothing.

"What's up with him?" he said.

"He's not speaking to you. You said you'd take him to the Science Museum."

"Did I?"

There was the clatter of plates and a creak and groan and moan as he struggled to sit up in his chair.

"You promised," I said.

He gave a big sigh and said he couldn't make it as far as the Science Museum but he promised faithfully, absolutely faithfully, without fail, cross-his-heart and hope to die, to take me to RAF Hendon round the corner just as soon as Almost had fixed his car.

"He's fixed it!" I yelled, jumping up and down. "He's put a new tyre on!"

"Has he?" He stared blankly at me. He forgets things, does Grandad.

His face cleared. "Oh yes! Of course. I forgot. How stupid of me. Then we can go to RAF Hendon."

"That car," mum muttered.

Grandad gave her one of his looks. "What do you mean? That car?"

"Your Grandad can't go out Des and that's flat," she said.

Grandad heaved himself out of his chair, looked as if he was about to fall, then, as mum grabbed his arm, stood up. "If that car is starting," he said, "so am I. I am taking that child to Hendon."

Adults. You just have to wait.

He found his coat, his hat and his scarf. We went out. He double-locked the door, then he remembered he had forgotten his wallet and we went inside to look for it.

"Your heart, Dad," Mum said.

"My heart?" Grandad said. "What's wrong with my heart?"

"You know what the doctor said. Please Dad."

He gave her one of his beaming smiles. Grandad sort of doesn't hear you when he doesn't want to. "If I make a promise I keep it, don't I Des?"

"Yes, Grandad," I said.

He found his wallet. It was full of that month's money. Mum told him to leave most at home but he put it in his back-trouser pocket, saying it was safer with him. If he put things down in that house he never found them again.

He opened the door, lifted his head and gave a long, deep sniff. That's what air smells like, he said. I haven't smelt air for a long time. Wonderful stuff. Air.

Mum closed her eyes. She said she didn't believe in God, even though she seemed to believe in the vicar now because she saw him quite a bit, but I'm sure she began to pray that the car wouldn't start. Grandad stepped off the step without knowing it was there. He would have fallen if mum hadn't grabbed his arm. She glared at me. I beamed back at her. I was going to RAF Hendon! To fly a Spitfire!

Stewart in my class hadn't flown one! I grinned at the thought of telling him. My smile slowly went as

Grandad pressed the button on the car key and nothing happened. The door wouldn't open. Don't worry, Des, he said. It always works manual. He put the key in the door lock and turned it one way, then the other. Nothing. Hmm, he said, scratching his head

"Are you sure you've got the right key dad," mum said.

"Women," Grandad said to me. "This car has its tricks, its ways, pecu-li-arities, do you know the word pecu-li-arities, Des?"

"Tricks, ways," I said.

He beamed at me. "That's right. Clever feller you have there, Jess."

"Don't tell me,"she said, giving me another glare.

He peered at the door, dented by a long, rusted scrape. "I'll remember the eccentricities of this door in a minute," he muttered. "Eccentricities, Des?"

"Pecu -li -*arities,*" I managed.

"Remarkable feller," he said. "Now." He spoke to the door. He speaks to things, does Grandad. "You won't defeat me," he said.

He put the key in, pulled it a little way out and then, with a strange upward movement heaved. The door creaked and groaned, suddenly swinging back on its hinges, knocking Grandad backwards. Mum only just caught him and she almost fell and I could see how angry she was but at the same time, that's what's so funny about grownups, she smiled when I jumped up and down in excitement and Grandad smiled at the car, his car, patting it as if it was a favourite dog or a cat.

"Let me drive, dad," Mum pleaded. He didn't hear her. Or didn't seem to. He was too busy adjusting himself to fit into the car. His car. Mum strapped me in and got in.

Grandad turned the key. The engine made a strange grating noise. Mum sighed and settled back in her seat, looking hopeful. Grandad scratched his head, fiddled and turned the key. The engine started and the car leapt forward, heading for the gatepost at terrifying speed. I screamed, shutting my eyes. When I opened them the car was bumping down the road. "Sorry about that folks," he said. "Your feller has made the gear a bit too sharp for me."

Mum's face was white. "Just, just take us to the local shops Dad," she said. "You don't want to go to Hendon do you Des?"

"No no," I said but my words must have been lost in the grating of gears and the blare of horns as Grandad went out on to the main road. A lorry passed him the driver mouthing words down at him. Grandad beamed up at him, raising his hand. The driver shook his head, but smiled. Grandad has that effect on people. Mum started to say something, but when he turned to look at her a van blared.

"Nothing dad, nothing," she said. She gripped my arm so tight it hurt.

"Amazing how things come back to you," Grandad said.

There was a long screech of tyres. But it wasn't Grandad. He had been driving ok for a bit. He had stopped at lights and was starting to go again when his lights went green. A car tried to cross when his lights were changing to red. There was no time to shut my eyes as I saw us heading for the other car. Our tyres screeched and slid and sounded as if they were going to come off. The other car flashed past us, inches from our headlights.

Grandad shook his head. "Some drivers," he said. "First thing you ever learn, Des. Both feet out."

Grandad took us into the huge hall full of aeroplanes and almost as full of children. It seemed as if every child on school holiday wanted to go to Hendon. My hated enemy Stewart had of course, made models of the Spitfire and Messerschmitt, but that was nothing compared with having a Grandad in the war.

"He wasn't in the war," mum said. "He did national service after the war. And you hated it, didn't you dad. You've told me that often enough."

"Well, you know," he said. "It was active service. Singapore. Fighting terrorists in the jungle."

"You fought terrorists in the jungle," I said. Wait until Stewart hears this, I thought!

"You were bored out of your mind, weren't you?" Mum said. "Air traffic control, mainly playing cards. Where you learnt to play bridge."

"Well, you know." Grandad said. It was funny. He seemed to grow a bit taller as we walked round the huge, echoing hall. "Oh my goodness." he said. "Look at that. A German Dornier bomber. Main plane that bombed London. When I was a kid I picked up a bit of one, shot down."

My mouth dropped so far open I thought I would never close it. "You shot down a German plane!"

His mouth dropped open too. "No no no," he laughed.

I had never seen him laugh like that before, at least for a long time. He had a crinkly mouth and his eyes and his whole body shook. Mum joined in. "Tell us when you shot down a plane dad," she said. "Go on."

Then I saw it. Spitfire 10 K. That was the plane that saved London, Grandad told us. He was wearing a crumpled peaked cap and took it off.

"Without it, I might not be here," he said.

"Nor me," mum said. "Or you."

Grandad wandered under the aircraft, staring up at the wings, the propellor, as if it was something in a church. There was a notice. *Ten -pounds - to - sit- in - a - Spitfire*. Oh please, please - I began, turning to mum to see her shaking her head. I turned to Grandad. "Don't you dare!" mum said.

I folded my arms and pushed out my lips. More than anything else in the whole world I wanted to sit in that Spitfire. At those controls.

Grandad was looking at us, fumbling at his back pocket, drawing out his wallet.

"No no, dad," mum said. "Don't be ridiculous!"

"My treat," he said.

"You don't want to go in that plane, do you Des," she said. "Ten pounds to sit in a seat!"

Grandad looked like a fighter pilot, jaw sticking out. "It's not just *sitting in a seat*," he said. "Women. They don't understand, do they, Des?"

As he took a ticket from the young man in Hendon uniform he shouted: "Outside, twenty-two flight!"

The young man grinned and saluted: "Welcome aboard, sir."

He showed the two of us up the shaky metal ladder to a rickety platform level with the door of the Spitfire's cockpit. Grandad lifted me up. "Careful dad," mum shouted as he staggered, first to one side, then to the other. I felt myself slipping in his hands. The ground dipped and swayed below me. His grip squeezed tightly on my armpits but he managed to heave me up and drop me in the pilot's seat.

"Are you all right, dad?" Mum yelled above the throbbing of the aircraft engine.

He panted for breath, grinning down at her.

"Chocks away!" he shouted.

Mum was with a small group, gathering round, gazing up. One of them was a young man with a tattered jacket and the tattoo of a snake creeping up his neck. "Chocks away," he shouted back.

"This yours?" the young man in Hendon uniform said. He held out a wallet. Grandad took it, thanked him and beamed at him, his face shining . "My goodness! This brings it all back to me."

"Were you in the air force?" the young man asked.

"He shot down a German fighter," I said.

The young man gaped at him. "Did you really, sir?"

"Well ... You know ..." Grandad began ...

"Is this the gear lever?" I said.

"Joystick!" Grandad said.

I made the sound of rattling machine gun fire. The man with the snakes on his throat pretended to dive underneath us and fire back at me. Get him Des, Grandad shouted, get him! Oh my God mum said, but beginning to smile. I felt I was flying as Grandad pointed to the clocks, the fuel, the speed, the landing gear.

"I was in air traffic control. National Service Singapore," Grandad told the Hendon man. "Boring mostly, but you know, sometimes ..."

The Hendon man gave Grandad a helmet and goggles and he put them on me. I felt as if I was flying through clouds as Grandad's voice sounded different, as if he was in a film.

"Changi Tower, Changi Tower, Changi Tower, Victor Sugar Sugar Charlie, can you read over?"

"Sugar Charlie, strength two. Fly past tower for visual ... You are one wheel up, one down ... clear landing gear, belly land on grass ..."

"Sugar Charlie."

I was shaking. I really felt I was crash landing on grass. My head banged on something. I was in a daze as I was lifted from the seat by the man in Hendon uniform who said: "Perfect crash landing sir. I wish you did this for us regular." We went down the metal steps, the small group below clapping and cheering.

"Fantastic," said the man with a tattooed snake, slapping him on the back.

"All right dad," Mum said.

He beamed at her. "All right? Feel better than I've done for years! Need a drink though."

There was a cafe next door and his hand patted one back trouser pocket then the other. "Oh dear," he said. Must have dropped my wallet again." He went back to the Spitfire but returned to tell us it wasn't there.

"It's not just the money he said, All my cards, mementoes, everything!"

"*Must* be there somewhere," Mum said.

"No," I cried. It's funny how you sometimes see things after they have happened. I didn't see him take the wallet, but I remembered Snake-Man slapping Grandad on the back then his hand slipping down and thinking it a bit funny.

"I've seen Snake-Man here before," said the man in Hendon uniform. "He goes in the direction of crowds. The next big one is the German Luftwaffe."

"Don't do anything stupid," Mum said, but that's the last thing you say to fighter pilots as we ran towards the German Luftwaffe.

"There he is!" I yelled, running towards the stand. Grandad ran with me . He beat me. I couldn't believe it! His legs pumped up and down, his face red and sweating. Snake-Man turned, his mouth dropping open. He had money in one hand and the wallet in the other. He flung the wallet away from him and ran. Grandad dived between two people, almost knocking them down, grabbing hold of his wallet.

"You are a pair of idiots," Mum began, panting up to us.

"Women," Grandad said. "After National Service, Des, I joined the Police and I ... " He held up his wallet, a triumphant grin on his face. The grin slowly went. A puzzled look crept over his face. Slowly, steadily, his legs crumpled and he fell into a heap on to the ground, his hand still gripping tight hold of his wallet.

The man from RAF Hendon was on a phone getting medical help. Mum was kneeling by Grandad, holding him. He coughed and a little dribble of sick trickled from his mouth.

"Pull his legs out Des," mum said. They were heavy and one was twisted under him so I couldn't move it. Someone helped me. Grandad looked at me and yet didn't look at me. His face was like paper and there were tiny bits of spit shining on his lips.

The ambulance will be ten minutes the man from Hendon said. Mum looked away for a second then kept talking quietly to Grandad but his body began to jerk in a funny way and the wallet dropped from his hand and then he was as still as if he was asleep except his eyes were staring open.

"Can anyone help?" mum shouted. People walked past or stopped and stood there staring. "I don't know if I can remember," she said. "Was a nurse but didn't finish ...."

She knelt over him and unbuttoned his shirt. A button came off Grandad's shirt and rolled to my feet. I picked it up.

A group of children passed, yelling. Mum locked her hands together in one position. Then another. She went to one side of him, leaned forward on his chest, pressing down with her locked hands again and again and again.

Grandad was as still as a log.

Mum stopped, gasping for breath, head drooped. Then started again. She looked a blur as she pushed down, harder, harder, faster, faster. Grandad's eyes flickered. He moved. He gasped as if he had been running all over again. A hand came on to mum's shoulder and someone pushed a funny-looking mask on to Grandad's face.

In a hospital bed Grandad was propped up. He gazed at the wallet and the shirt button I had brought him.

"Thanks Des," he said. Then he looked at Mum. "Thanks, Jess." She squeezed his hand.

"Women," she said.

Torture

Dirt. Oil. Grease. Why don't grown-ups like it? Well. Most grown-ups. The first time it happened was when Almost collected me. I thought my teacher, Miss Hancock, was going to send for the police. Mum always collected me from school but that day she was late. And later. Then I was the last one there. Then, the man that came was so black with oil and dirt, even I wasn't sure it was Almost, until I heard the surly grunt of his voice calling me to come on.

Almost was now working full-time at the garage for Mike. Miss Hancock asked me if I knew him. He's sort of - my dad, I said. Almost.

When Miss Hancock still stopped him, his hand moved so rapid I thought he was going to give her one but he pulled a letter from his overalls.

It was from Mum. She was now working at the hospital. After saving Grandad's life she was learning to become a proper nurse. She mended people as Almost mended cars.

What happened to my real dad I never knew. Whenever I asked mum she said he's in Australia. I hope.

That day, when Almost collected me the first time, he hadn't finished work and took me back to the garage.

"Stand there Des," he said. "Don't cross that line."

Funny. Before that day he'd never called me by my name. Just kid. Or you. Or worse.

I watched him go under the bonnet. There was a noisy, whining, grating noise. He forgot he told me not to cross the line. He gave me a spanner to hold, then told me to pick the right screw. It was magic listening to the screech of a gear vanish to a soft hum. This started to happen once a week. He would collect me on Friday and I would get home almost as filthy as he was. Mum would be very cross with me but somehow also pleased. Sometimes he was like a dad now, but sometimes like a big brother, for when mum read me a story he would listen and look at the words as if they were puzzles.

One night she said to Almost why don't you read him a story? I was in a bad mood and said he can't read. He got up and I thought he was going to go for me. So did mum who put her arms round me. Then he slammed out of the flat.

She pushed me away. "What did you say that for?"

"Because it's true," I said.

"Of course it's not true," she said. "He's a bit slow. That's all."

I stuck my lips out for sometimes adults don't see what is right in front of their eyes. Or what they don't want to see. Now I could have mum all on my own. I was glad he was gone. Glad glad glad. I knew he would come back pissed from the pub. I told her to put the bolt back on the door so he couldn't get back in.

"Don't you dare talk to me like that Desmond," she said. She stood over me, shaking, angry. She always calls me Desmond when she's really angry.

I was crying, crying. "Finish my story, finish my story finish ...!"

"Not until you say you're sorry."

I wasn't sorry. How could I say I was sorry when I wasn't? How could I? The flat door flew open. My door was open and we saw him go into the kitchen.

Mum leant over me, speaking in a sharp whisper. "Of course he can read. Desmond. Say you are sorry."

I could see him approaching his fists clenched. I remembered the time he had really hit Mum. I started to pull the duvet over my head but Mum pulled it back. I couldn't open my mouth. I couldn't say anything. He is such a big man and he stood there in the doorway his face all red and twisted.

"I can't," he said. "He's right. I can't read. Its torture. When you don't make the right start. When you don't make *any* start. Torture. Everything is words. Everything. Words. Torture. I have to ask. Pretend. Pretend I've lost my glasses to find something in the supermarket. Forms. Pretend this. Pretend that. Pretend my hands sprained and I can't write. *I can't write*. Sign my name proper. Half my life is excuses. That's why ... well never mind that. That's why I get so far but can't hold down no job. Mike at the garage suspects. I get other people to do the forms because my hands are dirty. That sort of thing."

"Why don't you tell the garage owner?" Mum said.

"Tell him? Tell Mike?" He stared at her, his mouth dropping open in amazement, as big as his face, swallowing up his whole face.

"If your job is ok."

He sat down on the end of the bed. "My job *is* ok. Better than the others. I always know. Or guess. Because I've always put bits and pieces together instead of words."

"Then tell him," she said.

"Tell the boss? Don't be stupid," he shouted. "Then he *would* fire me!" He dropped his head in his hands, the whole bed was shaking.

One night he came back late and I woke to hear them shouting. I heard him say that on one job in the garage he fixed up the brakes wrong and there was almost a smash. He stopped picking me up at school and I was sorry for I loved going to the garage. Then - I couldn't believe it. Even though Almost was awful sometimes I couldn't believe Mum could be so rotten to him. When class was leaving I went to her. She didn't see me because she was talking so close to Mike, the garage owner, who had come to collect his son Stewart.

I heard her say to him: "He can't read."

Then Stewart came up and said to me your dad is going to be fired because he smashed a car.

He didn't smash a car and he's not my dad I said and we began to fight before Mike and my Mum pulled us apart. She was cross with me and I said - why did you sneak on him?

"I didn't sneak on him!"

"You did, you did! You told Mike he can't read!"

"I did not."

I stared at her. Adults are always telling you not to lie and then they lie themselves!

Then she said: "You never heard that. Do you understand? Don't you *dare* say anything to him!"

"Why?"

"Because Mr Clever you do *not* understand. You don't understand men. And neither do I."

I don't understand women. I don't. Well. Maybe I do a bit more than I did. Because this was on a Monday. One of those rotten Mondays. I expected Friday to be even worse when I saw Almost collecting me at school. He was in such a funny mood. He told Mum he had lost his temp job at the garage. I knew it was because Mum had sneaked on him, I knew it. I knew it! She looked rotten when he said it, really rotten. She gave me that warning look which said plainer than words - keep your big mouth shut!

Then he gave her the biggest smile I have ever ever seen. The very, very biggest most ginormous smile! It split his whole face wide open.

"Mike told me he didn't want me to be a temp," he said. "He said he wanted me to be permanent. *Permanent!*"

Then, Almost said, he gave me the forms. The forms to fill in! To *write* on! Sweat went out over his face. Those forms! I was going to turn it down. Turn it down! I was doing my usual. Making my *usual* excuses because of those forms! Then Mike said - I think you have problems with writing, don't you?

Almost's fists clenched. "I got so angry I almost clouted him. Then he said - why don't you take courses?"

"Courses?" I said. "Courses? What do you mean - *courses*?"

"Evening courses."

He stared out of the window as if it was a whole new world he had never seen before, the tower blocks, the motorway, the cars he could work on.

"I never knew you could do that." he said. "I never knew it. I never knew someone would let you work full-time without doing the forms and all the rest of it."

His eyes shone. "Mike said I was such a good mechanic if I could do the paper-work I could really get on. I don't know how he knew I couldn't read, but he spotted it."

I was going to tell him then. Say it was Mum but she shook her head all violent behind his back until I thought it was going to come off and she put her finger to her lips. I don't understand women. I don't understand them at all but I kept my mouth shut because Almost took us to the Palace Pizza to celebrate and Almost learnt to spell BBQ Pizza and Mint Choc Ice and I ate them.

Mr Magic

Almost reads almost everything now. Papers, menus, notices, my writing, five pound notes. Everything. Mum was on her evening shift months later when he took me to the Palace Pizza and he even read the word TOILET and spelt it out before he went in there.

While he having a pee I played a space game on his iPhone. A man came in and sat at the next table. He smiled at me. I didn't know him and just did my puzzle. He got up and stood over me.

"You're fast," he said.

I was trying to get my spaceman away from the Flying Dragon but I felt his breath on my neck and crashed.

"Can you do magic?" he said. He took out a 10p coin, closed his hand round it then flung it into my face. I ducked, dropping the iPhone.

"Give me the coin."

"I haven't got it," I said.

"Yes you have! It went down your shirt!"

"It never!"

He waved his hands in front of my eyes then dipped one in my shirt pocket and took out a coin. I stared at it. He moved his hands in a circle so fast they were a blur and took a coin from under my plate. Another from behind my ear.

I clapped my hands and laughed and shouted for him to do it again. He waved a hand again but this time towards the waiter, who seemed to appear before him. He said something to him and as the waiter left Almost came out of the toilet. He stopped still, his face white and staring as the man smiled at him. He rapped the table with his knuckles and said: "Three, four knock at the door."

He always said this, I found, when he greeted Almost.

"What's going on?" Almost asked.

"This little feller has been nicking my money," the man said.

"I never! I cried. He took another coin from my ear. I began laughing. "It must be tricks," I said. "Magic."

"Tricks?" Almost said. "Yes. Tricks. Mr Magic does tricks all right." He looked funny, his face even whiter. "Come on Des. We're going home."

"I haven't finished my pizza!" I said.

"I'll get a container," Almost said, turning to the waiter, who had a beer in his hand.

"Aren't you going to have a drink with an old friend?" Mr Magic said. He flipped a beer mat from the air and slipped it under the glass as the waiter put it down in front of Almost.

I grinned and clapped. "Did you used to work together?"

"You could put it like that," Almost said.

"He worked magic with cars," Mr Magic said. "I worked magic with money. Notes."

"He's just got a job at a garage." I said.

Mr Magic stopped waving and became very still. "Has he now," he said. "Has he really?"

"A *permanent* job," I boasted.

Almost left his beer unfinished. He pulled me up by the shoulder and hurried me off towards the car. The car was a garage one which Mike used for all kind of jobs. Almost shoved me into it and I saw Mr Magic writing down the name of the garage. As Almost was about to drive off Mr Magic knocked at my window. He was holding something in his hand.

Almost wound down the window. "You dropped your wallet, Steve," he said.

Almost drove away fast. He kept on looking in his mirror, as if someone was following him. "Who was that?" I asked. He didn't answer.

"He called you Steve," I said.

He didn't answer. He went a funny way home. A long way round. Very fast. At first it was great. Then I was frightened. He swerved as a van came out of a narrow turning and he had to swerve again the opposite way as a bus leapt towards us and he slid between two parked cars bumping, screeching, on to the pavement. He was an amazing driver. He had never driven that way before. There was a silence. He had forgotten to fasten my belt and I had been thrown into the seat in front of me, banging my head. Something in the car was rocking from one side to another. I could hear voices and then the car shot back and forward off the main road and parked in a quiet street.

He stared out of the window his hands gripping the wheel as if they were glued there. He seemed not to know I was there or hear me crying at first and then looked about him as if it was someone outside and saw me in the mirror as if he didn't know who I was at first.

Then he said: "Des, I'm sorry. I'm so sorry I wouldn't have hurt you for all the world I thought ... I don't know what I thought ... what I was doing ... "

There was a trickle of blood coming from the bang on my head. He got the medicine box out and put a plaster on. It wasn't much. It was the fear more than anything. I liked him being soft with me but I hated it as well, I don't know what I thought.

"Why did he call you Steve?"

He stiffened. He seemed to become that strange person again. Just for an instant. "Don't call me that again. I'm not that. You never heard him say that. You never saw him. All right?"

Always people are telling me I didn't hear things. See things. Is that what growing up is?

A few days later, when Mum had just picked me up from school and was talking to some friends I saw Mr Magic at the school gates. He smiled and took a coin from his mouth. He seemed to be made of coins. You couldn't help watching him, walking towards him.

"Hello young man," he said. "Des, it is Des isn't it? He tossed a coin in the air and it vanished. Into the air. "Is Steve picking you up?"

"His name's not Steve," I said.

"Oh. What do I call him?" His smile broadened and his eyes seemed to grow larger.

I backed away. "I haven't heard you say this," I said. "Haven't seen you."

"Haven't - Oh." He laughed until his body shook. " I see."

I heard Mum shouting and that broke the spell and I ran.

"Why don't you come when I call you?" she said. "I've been shouting for ages!"

"There was this man."

"What man?"

I pointed. There was no-one at the gates. He had vanished. Like his coins. Disappearing into the air. I almost pulled her by the arm through the gates. There was no sign of him. Only people we knew pushing scooters and chatting and children chasing one another, and cars inching their way into traffic.

"What are you talking about, Des?"

"There was this man."

She looked around sharply. "What man? Who? Who are you talking about?"

"The sort of man you haven't seen. You don't hear what he says."

She sighed and took my hand. "Come on Des. I have no idea what you're talking about. You're always making up funny stories now. You're made of stories, aren't you."

It was a Friday. It always seemed to be Friday when things happen. Almost picked me up. He was late because people were going away for the weekend and wanted their cars done.

"Everybody wants their cars done yesterday," Almost said. Funny that. How can you have your car done yesterday?

He left me in the garage office with his iPad to play a game while he finished a car. The computer went wrong. I couldn't fix it and went to find him.

I loved the oily smell, the clanging, the music, men whistling. He was doing the battery of a car, revving it, powering it into life. I shouted to him but he didn't hear me because of the roar. As it died I was about to shout again but I saw the man on the other side of the car.

Mr Magic.

"We need the best engine. The best driver. You're the one Steve," he said.

The engine roared. Almost turned to look into it, inches from me. I ducked behind it, trembling.

Mr Magic's hands were in his pockets, his face smiling. It was a posh car he was driving. A BMW. "This job's the big one," he said.

"The next one's always the big one," Almost said, connecting the battery tightly. He looked around. "What did I do with those clips?"

"Are these what you're looking for?" Mr Magic took a number of clips out of the air. He seemed to make them out of air. One clip. Another. I half-stood up staring. Almost turned. If I had not dropped quickly he would have seen me.

"Who was that?" he said.

"What? Who?" said Mr Magic.

"I thought I saw someone."

Almost came round the car and I just managed to slip behind the next one, trembling.

"There's always something, someone," Mr Magic said. "You're a bag of nerves, Steve, on that tinpot salary of yours."

My foot touched a spanner.

Almost's head jerked up sharply. Mr Magic laughed. "See what I mean? A bag of nerves."

"It may be tinpot money," Almost said, "but its honest money." He took the pay packet from his jeans pocket, brought out a bundle of notes then stared at the pay packet and payslip as if they were even more precious than the notes themselves.

Mr Magic laughed. "Imagine. Not having to work again. Not having to worry about money ever. Imagine!" He flicked his fingers in the air and ten pound notes appeared in his hand. Almost gaped at them.

"And that little feller," Mr Magic said. "Des is his name, isn't it? Could be very useful. A kid his size. A kid so smart." A shiver went down my back, made my legs tremble. Me? Smart? Is that what I was? Smart! I stared up at the money. Imagine, I thought. Imagine! Money. Money out of air. I could buy Mum things. I could find my proper dad. Go to Australia and look for my proper dad!

Almost looked at the car bonnet. His money had gone. He snatched them back, wedged them in his pay-packet and stuffed it in his pocket.

Almost's fists clenched. They seemed to swell larger. I had never seen him so frightening. "Don't you dare go anywhere near that kid," he said. Mr Magic backed away from him, the heels of his shoes inches from my face. Mr Magic held his hands up. "All right, all right, all right," he said. "All right. But I need your help. You don't want Mike - it is Mike who runs this company isn't it? - to learn about that company you borrowed money from and never paid back to, do you?"

Almost's fists seemed to grow smaller. Mr Magic smiled. He squeezed Almost's shoulder. "All I need is you to soup up a car, Steve. That's all."

He opened his other hand. In it was a ten pound note. "You forgot one," he said.

I was asleep in the car reception office when Almost woke me up. Was what had happened something I had dreamed? Or made up? I was so muddled about what was life, and what was story, what was real, and what was story, that Almost had to lift me up and carry me to the car. I closed my eyes again. Tightly. It was nice. Nice. Being a baby again. I wanted to be a baby again. Growing down. Until I was in the yard. Then I heard a car starting. Driving it away was Mr Magic. He gave me a big smile and waved. You couldn't help grinning back at him and waving back and I remembered what he had said.

"Can I be smart?" I said.

Almost stopped so suddenly I dropped from his arms and fell. He stared down at me. "What did you say?"

"Can I be smart? Useful?"

His look changed so I was really frightened. It was like the look he gave Mr Magic. He pulled open his car door. "Get in".

"He's the man I don't see," I said.

"That's right. You still don't see him. Understand?" He slammed the car door shut on me. "Do you understand?"

I almost didn't want to know. I almost wanted him to be real. Mr Magic. For ten pound notes to really come out of the air. But of course Clever Clogs Stewart in my class knew about it. Or at least how to make twopence come out of an empty glass. I showed Mum while she was doing supper. I put a piece of white drawing paper on the table with a coin on it, put an upturned glass on it and the coin vanished. My goodness, she said. How did you do that?

"I watched Mr Magic in the garage," I told her.

She went very quiet.

"Why am I not supposed to see him?"

"Never you mind".

"Can he disappear?"

"I wish he would," Mum said.

"Why?"

She was suddenly angry. "Will you stop asking questions Mr Clever?"

"Why?"

"Why why why?" She thumped her fist on the table. "You're always why why why!"

She didn't often get so angry. I was frightened. A smell of burning came from the kitchen. It was the eggs she had scrambled. She told me I'd have to eat them because there was no more and when at bedtime she said what story did I want and I said one about Mr Magic she got angry all over again and I got no story at all and I thought I would never get to sleep but I did. Dreaming about Mum arguing with me only it wasn't with me. It was with Almost. And it wasn't a dream. I could hear them through the wall.

"You promised me you'd never see him again!" Mum said.

"I'm *not* seeing him, Almost said. I'm seeing his car. I can't stop him bringing a car into the garage, can I?"

"You can get someone else to do it."

"All right."

"Promise?"

He said he would promise but the next time he picked me up from school he went back to the garage. "Stay in the car," he told me. I heard a bang. Then another. They were such terrific, crunching bangs I couldn't stay away. I crept towards the noise.

And stared.

And stared. Almost wasn't mending a car. He was breaking it. He ran a chisel along the length of it. Kicked at the panel of the door. When he pulled it open the door creaked and groaned and tilted on its hinges.

"Good," someone said. "Very good".

It was Mr Magic. It was as if he came out of the air with a flick of someone elses fingers. He ran his fingers over the peeling bonnet and the battered door as if they were made of gold. Almost got in the car and started it. At first I couldn't hear nothing. Then a low throbbing. Then the sound like an aircraft taking off. Then it went down to an almost silent mutter. Almost opened the bonnet. Then sun glittered off a gleaming metal engine. Mr Magic grinned and stuck up his thumb. I ran back to Almost's car and pretended to be asleep. As Almost came back to the car I heard Mr Magic say : "At the main used car dump. It's not coins that come out of the air. It's NOTES. "

All the kids know the main car dump. You can see it from the playground in the park. Cars swinging in the air before they're crushed.

The following Friday Almost picked me up from school and took me to the playground. He brought my scooter out of the boot and left me with Madge, a mum who had a number of us. She thought I was scooting in a race round the park but I sneaked back to the car and hid in the boot.

I could hear the great banging and crashing as cars were crushed like cardboard boxes at the dump. I got out of the boot. I followed Almost. People thought I was with him. If he turned I dodged away so he couldn't see me.

Almost went into an office to book in the car he had battered. It looked empty, but I saw a thumb coming up from the back. The battered car was on rails behind others. I could see what they were up to. Mr Magic would get through the security gates then drive to the pay office where they were counting out the notes.

I didn't know what to do. I wanted to tell the office man there was going to be a robbery. But if I did they would arrest Almost. I knew he didn't really want to do it but Mr Magic had him in his clutches.

I watched behind a file cabinet as the office man pressed a button. The security gate opened for the next battered car. He pressed another button. A giant squeezer pulled up the car. It squashed it one way. Then another. When the office man let open the security gate to let the car with Mr Magic in it through, Almost gave him a form to sign.

I saw Mr Magic scramble into the driving seat. In another few seconds he would be at the pay office. I ran forward and hit the buttons as Mr Magic went for the starter. The engine roared but as it leapt forward the giant tweezers clamped round the back. The car roared then screamed with pain as the tweezers began to swallow it. It looked as though Mr Magic had lost his Magic but, although the giant tweezers ripped off part of the boot he gunned the superb engine Almost had put in and just escaped through the closing gates.

I thought he was going to give Almost no trouble ever again. But I was wrong. Very very wrong.

THE END

My goodness! You have written an exciting story, Des, Miss Hancock said. Do you know, at times I almost believed it was true!

Of course, I couldn't say nothing, could I? Neither could Almost. But the following Friday when he came to collect me from school we knew what Miss Hancock was staring at in the local paper, although she finally decided not to say anything either. The headline on the front page was: ESCAPING MAN ALMOST CRUSHED IN CAR DUMP.

Grandad's Fridge

When Grandad picked me up from school we always had a race. We were four floors up. There were twenty floors altogether. One of the lifts was broken. Grandad kept pressing the button but the other seemed to be stuck at floor twenty. Maybe someone was loading things. He waited for the lift and I ran up the stairs. I was done in from football and by three floors I was walking. By four I was gasping for breath. When I reached our door the working lift had only just started going down. After that climb I deserved something, I thought.

I pulled open the fridge door. A drift of smoke or something came out. I coughed. Waved it away. Amongst all the clutter I could see my shepherd's pie. I opened the freezer. There were just two choc-ices left. I went to take it then heard the lift. I went to the door. The lift had just reached the bottom. I saw stuff in the fridge had begun to melt. The choc-ice was dribbling chocolate. I couldn't let it waste, could I?

I ate it, lick by delicious lick.

There was the clunk of the lift and the slide of the door before Grandad came in. "This block of flats!" he said. "When are they going to mend those second lifts?" He sniffed. "What's that smell?" He went into the kitchen. He opened the fridge.

"Have you been in here?

"Me, Grandad?"

He picked up the stick which had carried my choc-ice. I had never thought before he could be a policeman. He looked straighter and bigger and as if he was about to arrest me.

"Just answer me, Des! Was it open when you came in?"

I was frightened. I was about to be arrested for stealing a choc ice! I shook my head.

"What was it like?"

"L-like? Like a choc - ice."

"Not the choc-ice! The fridge! Stuff in it is melting ... Was this fridge door open when you came in?"

"No ... There was a bit of smoke or something ..."

"Smoke? Was anything hot? Did you see any flames?"

"Flames?" Was he going funny? I'd heard mum say that to Almost.

"Pull that plug out!" he shouted. " I can't bend very well ... Pull it out, Des!"

I had to crawl on my hands and knees under a shelf to do it. Panting for breath he dragged out the fridge. He looked at the back. He took out my shepherd's pie, eggs and felt at the inside back.

He pulled me to the door. I had never seen Grandad move so fast. The lift was still at our floor and we shot down to the Warden's office. Mr Bottomley was a big fat man who was always on his phone. He didn't like Grandad because he was always complaining about the lifts.

"They're getting sorted," he said. "Next week." Mum and her friends called him Mr Next-Week.

"Fridge. Fire hazard," Grandad said.

Mr Next-Week jumped up faster than I believed possible. "On fire?"

"Des saw smoke."

"Des." He fastened his eyes on me. I was trouble. Mainly about my bike. Mr Next-Week liked notices. He put them everywhere. One of his favourites was BICYCLES LOCKED ON THESE RAILINGS MAY BE REMOVED WITHOUT WARNING. Mine had been removed and I thought I was never going to get it back.

As the three of us went up in the lift, Grandad said: "It was a fridge that caused the Grenfell Tower fire wasn't it?"

"Mmm," Mr Next-Week said.

A fridge? Causing a fire? I thought fridges were always supposed to be cold things. When the lift clunked to a stop I looked through the window towards the motorway. There was the covered tower block with a green heart at the top. Grenfell Tower. I didn't know much about it. I must have been five when the fire happened. I was woken up one night. There was a frightening clatter of sirens. Mum's bed was empty. I called out but she didn't reply. There was a noise in the corridor near the lift. She was in a little crowd trying to see through the window. She lifted me crying. I just saw something like a big huge candle burning near the motorway before she took me back to our flat and we slept the rest of the night together.

Now, when we went into the flat, Mr Next-Week examined the fridge. The frost in the fridge was melting and there was a pool of water on the floor. "You're going to lose the food from this freezer," he said.

"Thank you," Grandad said. He looked taller, hands clenched, not very Grandad at all. "It was a Hotpoint that caused the Grenfell Tower fire wasn't it?" he said.

"Mmm," Mr Next Week said. "Earlier models than this. All these were checked."

"It felt to me it was overheating. Stuff in the freezer is melting."

"Was it left open during the day?"

"It was closed. Wasn't it Des?"

"Who took you to school, Des?"

"Almost."

"Do you remember whether the fridge door was closed, when he took you to school, Des?"

I shook my head. Grandad never trusted Almost about anything. They both looked at me. It was Des again. I felt it from the looks on their faces. "I had to eat the choc-ice. It was half-melted."

Mr Next-Week sighed. He patted the fridge as though it was a pet dog. "I've had no complaints about any of the other fridges, sir. I suggest you replug it and check it again."

I pinched that second choc-ice before it all melted but I never got that shepherd's pie. I had some spaghetti green stuff I hated and Almost put me to bed because Mum was held up at the hospital. I woke because of arguments. It felt like the middle of the night but Grandad was still there. My tummy felt bad. I cried out but nobody came in.

"I've just plugged the fridge in, Dad," Mum said. It sounded as though she had just come back.

"Well you can unplug it," Grandad said. "I'll buy you another."

"There's plenty of other things I'd rather have."

"I checked it," Almost said.

"Are you an expert?" Grandad said.

"Are you?"

They looked as though they were going to get into a fight. All over a rotten stupid fridge! As I stumbled out of bed I saw Mum make Almost sit down.

"No ..." Grandad was saying. "But I know how many people were killed at Grenfell ..."

Mum saw me and came across. "Please dad! A child is trying to get to sleep!"

So I got a cuddle from Mum which I had been missing while she was on late shift. "Tell me ..." I began, all sleepy.

"You've had your story, kid," she said.

"Tell me another ... Tell me what happened at Grenfell ..."

"You don't want to hear about that!" she said all sharp which of course made me want to hear it much more.

"There's Gangsta Granny ..." said Mum, grabbing the first book she found.

I remembered that big candle, lighting up the night-time sky. The biggest bonfire I had ever seen, but it wasn't bonfire night yet.

"Where were we," Mum said, and began reading. "All that could be heard in Granny's bungalow was the ticking clock and - "

"Is that what happened to Tom?" I said.

I dunno what never made me think it. Realise it at the time. Why no-one ever told me then. Tom was my best mate. We used to get together against Stewart and Henry. He was a good scorer. Then one day I was just told he wouldn't be coming back to school. I dunno why you don't think. Wonder. But I never. I may even have thought it was mean of him to leave it to me to fight those two sods Stewart and Henry on my own. I dunno.

"Is it what happened to Tom?"

"... the ...the ... ticking clock and ..."

She wasn't looking at the book. She was looking through the window. At the burnt block covered in plastic. Her mouth was open but she seemed to have lost her voice. She kept staring out of the window. At the motorway. The traffic. We could hear the hum after hum of every car, the rumble of lorries, see the block, with the green heart and the words I couldn't read.

"What does it say?"

She swallowed. "Forever ..." She swallowed again. "Forever... in our hearts." She put the story down and pulled me to her. I could feel her heart beating. "Tom was ... was missing, love." Her voice was muffled against me.

"Could ours all burn up?"

"Of course not, kid!"

"Why not?"

"Because ... because ... it can't, it won't ... because ...they've looked at it all, all over again, they ... they've checked every ... "

"Mr Next-Week?"

Mum laughed, said well he does take his time doesn't he, drew the curtains together, snap - snap - snap, and went back to Gangsta Granny, the squeak of whose hearing aids reminded me of Grandad, or should I say Inspector Grandad, remembering how he arrested the old fridge as I drifted off to sleep ...

There was a second choc-ice. I must get it out before it melted. I opened the door of the fridge. Tom was there. Tom wanted me to pass to him so he could score. It wasn't a fridge. It was a fire. Burning hot, the flames licking round me, someone screaming. There were sirens screaming in my ears. Filling my ears. Hands reaching out for me. Or were they trying to push me further back into the fire? A woman's face. A woman with straggly hair. A witch. I couldn't scream no more. I thrashed with my legs and arms, thrashed and kicked but the woman was stronger than me and held me down until I was limp.

The woman gave me water. She became my Mum. I was so hot. I had wet my trousers.

"What on earth were you dreaming?" Mum said.

"Dunno." I said. I didn't want to remember. I didn't want to go back to school even though it was football, my fave day. I wanted to stay with mum but she had to go to work. I didn't even want to play football. I didn't want to be centre-half of my team where Mr Hunter put me. Boring. I wanted to be centre forward, where Stewart played in his team. Mr Hunter had put Mick there and I knew he was no good as a striker. It was raining a bit and muddy. I got the ball when Mick kicked off - well, you don't pass back if you're a striker do you? And I thought I saw Tom. Tom. Out there on our wing. I just stood there. Everybody was yelling at me. I didn't know where the ball was. I didn't know where anything was.

Stewart's hands were in the air. "Well scored, Stewart," Mr Hunter said. "Goodness! Early goal. One minute five. You all right, Des?"

All right? I didn't know if I was all anything. I struggled to keep myself together but that day I seemed to be slower than Stewart and he almost scored again a couple of times. They got a corner and I marked Stewart. As I rose in the air I saw Tom. I headed it towards him and fell in the mud as Tom ran forward. Boys were shouting, yelling. He'd scored! Tom had scored!

"Well done Des! Good pass. One all. Great run Mick. "

Mick. Of course. It was Mick who had scored. Not Tom. He hadn't got a great shot but he could run all right. One all. The next time they had a corner it was on the ground. Stewart had a clear shot at the goal. I could never reach the ball. I did a long, sliding tackle, whacking right into him, bringing the bastard down. The whistle shrieked. Mr Hunter was pointing at the penalty spot.

"I went for the ball!" I yelled at him.

He just gave me a look. He knows me, and I know him.

Stewart scored from the penalty. They won 2-1. In the dressing-room he gave me a finger. I would have given him one but I just sat on the bench. I didn't feel like doing anything, giving him anything while he chuntered on about how good he was and what he'd got that I didn't have until I told him I'd got a bigger newer, better, bigger fridge than what he'd got.

"Fridge?" he said, pulling on his trendy new trainers. "Fridge?"

It was the only new thing I could think of. I liked our new fridge. We called it Grandad's Fridge. It had a bigger, colder ice-cream compartment than the old one.

"Boring!" he said, snapping the catches on his trainers, patting them, so I could see how good they were. "He's got a new fridge!" he said to his mate Henry.

"Great! Wo-ho!" cried Henry, putting a pistol to his head. "A new fridge!"

I stood up, clenching my fists, feeling my whole face burn-up. "It is if your old one catches fire!" I yelled.

That got them. For a sec. They stared at me.

"Gerron!"

"Fridges don't burn!"

"It's one of his stupid stories," Stewart, said, turning away.

"It did in Grenfell! That's what caused the fire."

That shut them. But not for long. " Is yours going to go up like it?"

"Boomph!" laughed Henry.

"I'm ok. I'm in a house," Stewart said.

"So am I," said Henry. "A *house*."

I went for them then but Mr Hunter came in and grabbed me. It was Almost who collected me and Mr Hunter had what he used to call his quiet word with him. When Almost took me to his car he told me to keep my fists to myself. He had been too free with his fists when he was my age and where did that get him? I didn't listen and when he said did you hear me I didn't even nod my head.

When I sat in my seat and he told me to fasten my belt I wouldn't. Why should I do anything he told me? He wasn't my Dad. I wanted my Dad. I was going to find my real Dad. Why should I do anything that bastard Almost told me? When he clipped my belt I unclipped it. I thought he was going to belt me one. I wanted him to. I was going to have a go back at him. He pushed the window down and pulled out a cigarette.

"I'll tell Mum you had a fag."

He gave me a look then lit it and stared out of the window.

I coughed. It was horrible but I pretended to like it.

"Oh!!! ... Great! ... Can I have one?"

He smoked and took no notice of me until I got fed up and fastened my belt. Stuck in traffic, he made a detour, driving close past Grenfell. A bit of the cover was torn and I could see blackened walls. "Tom used to live there."

He nodded and smoked.

"I saw him today."

"You saw him? You ... imagined -"

"I *saw* him! ... Why did you come here?"

"Why why why Mr Why ... I dunno. There was a collection at work on the anniversary ... I dunno."

There was a lot of smoke on the motorway and I thought it was from one of the towers but it was just a big lorry and I was starving and Fourways Tower was there just like normal and there was always ice-cream after football. I wolfed down fish 'n chips, swallowing every scrap of batter and was drooling at the thought of the ice-cream.

But Mum said: "I told you. If you started another fight with Stewart and Henry there would be no ice-cream."

"They started it!"

"That's not what Mr Hunter told Almost."

I hated everyone then, including Mum. Particularly Mum because she wouldn't give me that ice-cream. She had promised me that ice-cream from the new fridge and I was going to have it. I opened the fridge. She grabbed me.

"Don't you dare."

I got a hand free but Almost came up from behind and pinned me down. "All right sunshine, all right."

I struggled and struggled until I collapsed, gasping for breath and he slowly released me. I was so done in I had to use the ledge of the window-sill to pull myself up. The room seemed to swing from one side to the other before it righted itself. Through the window, in the distance, I could see Grenfell.

"They said our flat would burn up like Grenfell."

She stared at me. "They never did."

"They did they did! You never ever ever believe anything I say but it's true! It's true they said it would go up Boom Boom Boom but *they* would be ok *they* live in nice houses, you would be ok in winter, you'll be warm, you'll have a nice fire."

Mum looked out of the window towards Grenfell. Towers near it glinted in the sun but Grenfell was covered. "Did you hear any of this, Almost?"

"No. But you know what they're like."

"What do you mean? What they're like?"

He shrugged. "What they're like."

She stared out of the window again. I wanted to watch the telly but there was something wrong with it. Almost said he was going to fix it but did nothing but stare out of the window. Mum picked up old leaflets that came through the letterbox.

"Fourways Tower Campaign," she said, passing a leaflet to Almost. "They want us to join their campaign to change this cladding now."

"Ten pounds a month!" he said. "You're joking!"

"Better than what might happen."

"Can't afford it." He opened the fridge.

"What might happen?" I said.

Mum said nothing. Almost took a can of beer from the fridge but just stood there with it in his hand.

"Could we burn down?" I asked.

"No! Well ... " We all looked out of the window.

"What happened there then?"

"There? Grenfell? Yes ... There was a fire but we all have to take care, don't we? Houses may burn down ..."

"But there are less stairs to run down. Less people to cause a fire," Almost said.

"They shouldn't have said that! That's really nasty of them." Mum was shouting, shaking. She put her arms round me. "I'll speak to Miss Hancock."

"I wouldn't. Make things worse." Almost played with the cap of the beer tin but didn't open it. "Des said he thought he saw Tom at football."

"Tom?" She squeezed me and hugged me and kissed the top of my head.

"Tom was at Grenfell, wasn't he?"

"Tom? ... Tom, yes ..." There were tears in her eyes. "Tom was ... Tom was lost there love. Yes, yes, he was ...."

She held me tight. There was a crack like a whip, like a gun going off. We both jumped, knocking a chair over. I don't know what we thought had happened but we saw it was Almost snapping the beer can. We laughed. We all laughed and laughed when we saw the amount of foam jumping out over his hands.

Almost licked it off and said: "Let him have his ice-cream, Jess."

I ate it lick by lick while Almost mended the telly and they let me have the telly later than usual to play Fantasy Football, Chelsea beating Arsenal three one until it was dark and as she carried me back to bed I could see the lit towers round the motorway except for Grenfell with its cover and I was asleep before she tucked me in.

Gotcha!

I dunno who called the dog Toby. I dunno who he belongs to or where he comes from. You can't have pets in the flats. FORBIDDEN it says. NO PETS ALLOWED in big letters.

I was in my pyjamas one night coming downstairs to help mum up with shopping when I saw him. Mum had got hot pizza for supper. Toby must have got in with mum, smelling the pizza, belly wiggling, long ears dangling.

He was at the foot of the stairs staring up at me. I told him it was pizzas and dogs didn't like pizzas but he came up a step and gave me another squeal putting his head on one side. There were bits of ham and I tore off some and chucked it. He went after it.

I don't know how he did it but by the time I reached our door he was there, cocking his head at me.

"You can't come in," I said. "They'll arrest you."

I'm sure he knew what I was saying. He padded over and rubbed his head against my legs. I turned him round and pointed downstairs. He looked at the stairs. Then he looked up at me. That did it. I had never had anyone look at me like that before, well mum of course, and Almost a bit. But no-one ever needing me like that. Wanting me.

"Des! Shut the door! It's freezing!" Mum opened the kitchen door. I pointed to my room and Toby shot like an arrow under my bed. Mum took the pizza. "You've been eating it," she said. "You really wolfed it down! Poor Des. You must have been starving. She sniffed. "What's that smell? Has that dog been in here?"

"On the stairs," I said, which was true. His tail swished out from under the bed and I pulled the cover down to hide it.

"Take them in the kitchen. I'll just make your bed."

I stood in the doorway, blocking it. "I'll do it mum."

She stared at me suspiciously. "Are you hiding something?"

I shook my head but she pushed past me and went into the room. Perhaps it was the sound of her voice that stopped the tail wagging. She stared around then hugged me and rubbed my head. "I'm sorry Des, but you're so often naughty, I can't believe it when you're good."

I smiled up at her. While she put the pizzas in the oven I pulled back the bedcover, discovering why there had been no movement under the bed. Toby was curled up there, head buried in his paws, full of pizza, tail wrapped round his bottom, fast asleep.

I stared at my pizza, most of which had been eaten by Toby. Mum was cutting into her whole pizza. Mine went down in three or four mouthfuls after the huge piece I had given Toby and I was still hungry, watching mum enjoying hers. So this was the reward for being good.

After that I pinched a few biscuits and began to feel sleepy, so sleepy that I forgot about Toby. Mum went to the bookshelf to pick out a story. It was not until

I stumbled into my room that I remembered Toby under my bed, fast asleep. I have never woken up so fast. I opened the window. Outside were ladders and planking where painters were working. Toby's eyes flickered open. I gave him a shove and he went out on to the planking. I slammed the window down pulled across the curtain and managed to get to my door before mum entered.

"What's the matter?"

"I - I'll read my own story."

"Are you sure?"

"Miss Hancock says we'll learn to read faster."

"Oh darling. Every night of your life I've read you a st - "

Toby gave a shrill, piercing whine. She pushed me to one side and looked round the room. I grabbed my music player and just managed to get it on to drown out the sound of the dog scratching on the window.

"I'm sure I heard that wretched animal in here," she said. "All right, darling. You're in such a funny old mood tonight, aren't you."

She tucked me in and kissed me. As soon as she'd left I opened the window partly and tried to shove Toby away along the plank where he could reach the ladder but he whined bitterly and I had to let him back in. We shared the biscuits and I told him a story.

"Once there was a dog called Toby ..." I dropped a biscuit on the cover and it was gone in a second. "He stole biscuits and wouldn't do what he was told ..."

I pointed to the open window but Toby went round in a circle three times at the bottom of the bed, shook himself, gave me a good-night look, curled up and went to sleep. It was as if he had slept there every night of his life. I curled up and was asleep before my eyes closed.

I heard Mum look into the room to check if I was ok when she and Almost went to bed. She wouldn't have seen Toby because my wardrobe hid him. In the morning when I woke up there was no Toby. The curtain flapped at the open window. For a moment I thought I had dreamed about Toby. Then I saw the circle he had made at the bottom of the bed and the wisps and lumps of hairs which I was careful to brush away. I gazed out of the open window. Toby was in the yard, having his breakfast at the bins.

No wonder everybody called Mrs Griffin Mrs Grumble. She grumbled about how old the paint was. Then when it was painted she grumbled about how the new paint stuck to her dress. She grumbled about my music player. But that was nothing compared with how she grumbled about Toby. She kept complaining to the Warden, Mr Next-Week, but Toby was used to hiding from him.

I saw Toby in the yard when Mum or Almost picked me up from school. He was all over me. We had pretend fights together but when I said "Down" he dropped down. One of the painters, Fred, had a dog and he taught me some training. I had my own Fetch ball. But nobody ever knew that he slept with me. I waited until mum and Almost thought I was asleep and leaned out of my window, gave a low whistle and snapped my fingers. The yard seemed empty for a time but then he appeared. I never knew where he came from, or where he went to during the day. He streaked silently up the painting framework and through my window. I put my fingers to my lips and he seemed to know he had to be quiet. He ate some biscuits and scraps of meat, slept until dawn and then vanished.

Until the painters left.

I never ever woke up until around seven. That morning it was just beginning to get light. Toby was whining. Was I awake or asleep? I could not keep my eyes open or my feet steady. He yelped. I must have trodden on his tail and banged my knee against the foot of the bed. I hopped about in pain and stopped suddenly staring, shivering. A wind was flapping the curtain in front of the open window, following Toby's gaze. There was no framework. No ladders. Toby stared down at a four floor drop and whined pitifully.

I slapped his bottom and put my finger to my mouth. I pointed to the fire escape at the corner of the building. Toby looked at me. There are times when a dog's look says everything. Would *you* do it? I put my arms round him and he snuggled his face into mine. A wave of tiredness ran through me and I was about fall into sleep again when I heard mum and Almost. They were both still in bed.

"I'm sure that wretched animal gets in..."

"Well you go ..."

"It's your turn..."

I shot down the bit of hall and opened the flat door. Toby was with me at the top of the stairs but immediately next to one of the rubbish bags people leave outside their door ready to dump. I grabbed him and we were down one flight then the next when a huddled shape came out of the darkness. I stumbled in fright and almost fell. Toby barked frantically.

"There he is! The little horror," Mrs Grumble cried, putting the corridor lights on as I ran to the bottom, letting Toby out.

This started a war in the flats, between those who liked Toby and those who wanted him put down.

"She says you let him in your room," Almost said.

"I never," I said. "I never! I just let him out of the building that's all."

Mum never said a word. She just gave me a couple of photographs. The first showed me in my pyjamas opening the flat door. The second letting Toby out.

"You shouldn't have let him in Des."

"I never let him in!" I shouted. "He just came in through the window."

She tried to hold me but I didn't want her to hold me. "They'll take him to the RSPCA darling," she said.

"What's the RSPCA," I said.

"Royal Society for the Prevention of Cruelty to Animals," Almost said.

"What's that mean?"

"They kill him."

I couldn't understand what he meant at first. I just stared at them and stared at Toby.

"They don't! You shouldn't say that to him!" Mum cried.

"Sorry. They put him down. But they do it without cruelty, Des. Well it's best to tell kids the truth isn't it? "

It was schooltime when Mrs Grumble brought up the pictures. I had Toby on the scarf I used as a lead. He looked at me so trusting. I wondered if he liked all the attention he was getting. At any rate, he wagged his tail at everyone, which made it worse. I undid the scarf I had fastened to his collar and yelled at him to follow me, half-jumping, half-leaping downstairs.

Mrs Grumble came out of her flat, falling back as Toby streaked between her legs. People were coming out of their flats, some swearing at Toby, some cheering. We jumped into the hall, Toby skating across a rug and banging into the wall. I had to jump up to reach the heavy door handle and I was just pulling it open with Toby's nose half-through it when the warden, Mr Next-Week slammed it shut.

"Gotcha yer, yer little bastard!" he yelled. I didn't know whether he meant me. Or Toby. Probably both.

It's funny, but I had a lovely day at school. There was football and I scored two goals and Miss Hancock asked me if I had a new story for her and I said Yes. About Toby. And I wrote about the race downstairs. She said what happened when Mr Next-Week shut the door and I said he escaped into the yard and she laughed said well that's naughty but nice Des. But when Mum picked me up from school he wasn't there.

"But he escaped!" I said.

"Darling," she said. "Listen ... Listen to me ... He's been taken away -"

I remembered. I was still in the story I wrote. The story I wanted. I remembered that morning. The thud of the door. The Gotcha. Mr Next-Week's horrible face. His horrible word. Gotcha.

"Killed."

"No darl -"

"Almost said - "

"Almost doesn't know. I talked to the man -"

"What man?"

"Somebody else will look after him darling. Somebody else will care for him."

The tears came. I couldn't stop. She tried to put her arms round me but I couldn't stop crying, hitting and kicking and screaming I don't want no-one else to have him! Toby is mine. He loves me! I love him! I want Toby I cried where is Toby where is he -

One of my kicks must have hit her on the leg because she cried out and hobbled away holding it and Almost pulled me off her and held me down on their bed until I could cry no more and couldn't move or speak. He held out a drink. I hit out at it and it flew in the air. I thought he would give me one. He has done. I would have hit him back. I was going to. But he just sat down on the bed.

"Suit yourself. These things happen, kid. It's life. L-i-f-e. Get used to it."

"Where is he?"

"Haven't a clue."

"Is he dead?"

"Dunno. Same thing happened to me once. Worse."

Worse? What could be worse? He told me. Almost was brought up in a care home.

"What's a care home?"

"A place where they don't care for you."

I sat up. Sometimes Almost made you laugh when there was nothing to laugh about. I think that's what mum liked about him.

Next to the care home, he told me, was a tumble down building site. On it was a mongrel everyone called Scruff. Like Toby, nobody knew where he came from but after evening meals kids took leftovers. Workers stopped them but, during visiting time, because Almost never had no visitors some of the workers let him sneak off. He was calling Scruff one evening and the dog was shooting across the pavement and a man with a brolly kicked out at him. Scruff bit him. Of course he did.

What did you expect? He bit him. The dog was caught and ... Almost sniffed and didn't speak for a bit. Then he said, said, well that was it. He never saw him again.

He put his arms round me and held me. I began crying again and he held me tightly like he had never held me before. Tightly as if he was going to squeeze me into him. Then he shoved me away.

"Now go and say sorry to your mum. Go and say sorry. Go on."

Suckers' List

Every morning, as I was taken to school by Mum, I saw the notice on the door of flat 28 on the floor below us, near the gleaming polished letterbox. There was a black warning hand with big red letters on it: NO Junk! NO Charity Mail! NO Free Newspapers! NO Unlicenced Callers!

When we were leaving the flats across the yard I glimpsed the grey hair and the sharp eyes of Mrs Grumble at her window. When you got back in the afternoon you felt she was still there, whether you could see her or not.

Grandad said nobody in our block needed a burglar alarm. They had Mrs Grumble.

One day, when Grandad was helping me build a Lego Wellington Aircraft, there was a knock at the door. I heard Mum asking Mrs Grumble in and I was sure I was in trouble. She had already complained about me leaving my dirty football boots in the passageway. She had a ringing voice

"I believe your father used to be a policeman?"

"Er ... Inspector ... he's er ... retired ...."

Grandad looked as if he wanted to hide, but there was nothing to hide behind but the half-finished Wellington Aircraft. Sure then it was the dirty boots she was complaining about I scrambled away and hid among the coats and my school things in the hall. I could just see Grandad being helped up by mum.

"Inspector Foster?" Mrs Grumble said.

Grandad stumbled, almost falling down again, gripped the table and managed to drop into a chair. It was a moment before he could get his breath back then he gave her one of his Grandad smiles.

"*Mr*, now I'm er ... glad to er ..."

"Inspector Foster, there have been robberies in this block of flats."

Grandad got back his breath. "That is a matter for pol -"

Mrs Grumble wore a black skirt and a dark blouse like a uniform. Her bracelets jangled as she talked. "I have told the police. They have done nothing. They are not what they used to be in your day."

Grandad shook his head, but he looked as if he agreed with her. She asked if he could give the flats help, advice? I didn't like this. I wanted Grandad to help me with my Wellington Bomber, and the very last thing I wanted was more Mrs Grumble. I went into the kitchen and found Mum was making tea and putting my favourite chocolate biscuits on a plate.

"You can't give them to Mrs Grumble!" I said. "She killed my dog!"

"Ssshhh!"

I nearly started crying all over again and she knelt and put her arms round me and said she knew, she knew it was awful but he wasn't my dog he was a stray -

"He was mine! He was my Toby!"

She clapped her hand over my mouth and held me for a bit and said there was always a Mrs Grumble wherever you lived in the world and you had to be nice to them and her proper name was Mrs *Griffin,* all right? I took the plate of biscuits and wanted to throw it at Mrs Grumble when I went in the room.

Grandad had got my best drawing pad and pencil to make notes with. He asked her to give him the number of the most recent flat where there had been a robbery. Her voice dropped to a mumble.

"Twenty-eight."

Grandad fiddled with his hearing aid. "I beg your pardon?"

"Twenty-eight," she shouted.

"Thank you. I can hear you," Grandad said, writing.

The biscuits slid all over the table as I put the plate down. I held up my hand like the warning hand she had on her letter-box. "But - but that's *your* number, Mrs Grum - " I caught my Mum's warning glance - "Mrs Griffin!"

She looked at me as if I was the one who had done the robbery. "You are quite right, Desmond. That is my number."

Grandad dropped his pencil, staring at her. I started to laugh. A sharp look from Mum stopped me. I gulped down the laughter but had to bite my lips to stop. Grandad stooped to pick up the pencil but I could see his cheeks quivering and he stayed there for a bit before he was able to speak.

"What ... er ... what exactly happened Mrs er Grum - er Griffin?"

There was a council letter about a gas leak in the building, she said. A man in overalls rang her bell later than day and said the leak was running through her property. She must leave while he checked the meter urgently. For a bit she stopped looking like Mrs

Grumble. She twisted her hands together, took a handkerchief from her sleeve and blew her nose. Mum went to her to put her arm round her but she stiffened and said she *had* smelt gas. She was *sure* there had been gas! She stayed only a few minutes with a neighbour -

She blew her nose again. She was not Mrs Grumble at all. She seemed to know what a fool she had been. She had lost her bag with a week's pension.

I put a biscuit on a plate and offered it to her. She stared at it. Mum started to steer me away, giving her a cup of tea but she took the biscuit.

"Thank you very much, Desmond."

Her eyes gleamed and there was a little laugh on her face which I think had not laughed for a very long time and Mum and Grandad laughed and I joined in although I had no idea what we were all laughing about.

"We will find the robber, Mrs Grum - Griffin, won't we Grandad?"

There was even more laughter which again I was not sure was all about as she bent to give me her hand to shake.

"Thank you, Desmond."

Was it a game, or were we after real robbers? I stopped wanting to be an aircraft pilot and wanted to be a policeman. After collecting me from school, Grandad took me to a pub near our flats called *Next Please*. He bought me a coke and said he would have a quick one, but it seemed like a very slow one to me. Then he met someone whom he said was Sergeant Wilcox, from the local police station, who shook me by the hand and said he had heard I was going to solve the crimes in my block of flats.

"I believe there's only been one," Grandad said.

Sergeant Wilcox shook his head. "We're very short of policemen, so PC Desmond would be a great help."

He drew out a piece of paper, crumpled and torn, which, he said had been found near the bins in the yard of our flats. On it was a heading which might have been scrawled there by a kid from our class: *SUCKERS LIST*.

"What's a sucker?" I asked.

"A sucker," said Sergeant Wilcox, "is someone like Mrs Griffin. Someone fooled, taken in by a thief." There was a list of numbers and names scribbled on the paper. "We think that the thief, who robbed Mrs Griffin, robbed others in the same block ..."

"Then sold the list to another thief ..." said Grandad.

"Correct. The victims usually are old, muddled or sometimes ashamed and don't report it."

I was jumping about with excitement at the thought of catching the robbers. "Can I report it?"

"Of course you can!" Sergeant Wilcox said. "We need all the help we can get!"

At a charity sale Grandad bought me a Cop's Uniform with a peaked hat and truncheon. Now I was in uniform I seemed no longer a nuisance causing trouble. Mr Next-Week, the Warden, also turned out to not only have a smile but a salute. He said if I was patrolling the block I should be sure to deliver all the robbers to him. But there were none. Not a single one. I went up and down to the sixth floor, was given rubbish to take down, asked if Almost would mend a car, told to pick up sweet wrappers and was about to take off my uniform when I saw him. Just as Mrs Grumble described him. Overalls. Big bag of tools. Boots. It was not a gas leak this time, he said, but water.

He had a crumpled piece of paper, exactly like the Sergeant had described - the Sucker's List! And the woman in number 95, Mrs Morgan, looked exactly like one of his Suckers: grey hair all over the place dithering about. He said he'd have to fix it before it got any worse but when I sneaked to the open door I couldn't see anything wrong. I couldn't see any signs of a leak.

He came out of the kitchen. He seemed to be looking directly at me. I was frightened and rushed to the cupboards at the top of the stair where there were brushes and cleaners. He took a step towards me. Mrs Morgan rushed out carrying her shopping bag, rushed back, grabbed her gloves and hurried down the steps. I watched this through a crack in the door. The man went back inside the flat, closing the door.

I crept out of the cupboard, picking up my toy truncheon, almost knocking a pail over. This didn't feel like a game any more. But there was the rattle of what might have been tools then silence. I crept up to the door and listened. I bent and peered through the letter box. I could see the man's bending face. He wasn't working in the kitchen at all. He had picked up a silver-coloured frame which I could see was a photograph of a friend of mine, Sam, in football clothes, smiling.

I ran, snatching up my truncheon, jumping over three or four steps at a time, almost falling once or twice, snatching at the rail, almost colliding into some people leaving one of the flats. I couldn't speak at first, gasping for breath as Mr Next-Week came out of what we used to call the Wardens Lair, a room at the bottom of the stairs. The usual scowl was set on his face and he was telling me to go slowly and carefully down the stairs until I got my breath and was able to speak.

"B ... B ..."

"What?"

Funny that you lose yourself, can't speak proper, gulping out words. "B ... Burg ... Thief . Nine ... number ninety five ..."

"Mrs Marsh?"

I nodded my head so vigorous I thought it was going to fall off. What shocked me most was I think he was more frightened than I was. He went white. He took out his iPhone, fumbled with it, dropped it, picked it up again, started to find a number, stopped.

"You saw him?"

"He said there was a water leak."

"Gas leak the other week ..." Mr Next-Week said. "Water now..."

He looked at his tie in a little mirror in the hut and I began to follow, truncheon in hand, to the lift. He told me not to follow, his finger quivering over number nine. He took his finger away and stared at me with something more like his usual frown on this face.

"Are you sure, Desmond?"

"I looked through the letter box! He was taking a photograph!"

His frown deepened. "A *photograph*?"

"It was in a silver thing."

"Frame."

He pressed the number and then, as the gates were closing, pressed the keyboard so they opened again.

"Did you see a knife?"

"Dunno. There was the clink of something as he put his toolbag down."

Before I could do anything he was out of the lift and pulling me over to his little flat and Mrs Next-Week was giving me a cup of milk which I hated and chocolate biscuits which were the best I ever tasted and Mr Next-Week was on the phone.

"Police ... Emergency break in ... Fourways ... Ninety- five ..."

Before I finished my last biscuit the screaming emergency was sounding and there was the screech of brakes in the yard and the clatter of police boots. Mr Next-Week went out to meet them and I picked up my truncheon but they wouldn't let me come which I thought was really rotten of them cos it was me who had caught him.

I didn't believe them at first. I thought they had let him get away. It was only when Mum came home I got the whole story. And it was only at bedtime that I believed it and it was awful. Awful!

The man *was* a plumber and he was Mrs Marsh's son. He was looking at himself, around about my age, in the photograph.

I couldn't look at anyone. I never wanted to look at anyone ever, ever again. I screwed up my police uniform and truncheon and shoved them right to the bottom of the waste bin. I buried my head in my pillow. Everybody was laughing at me!

"They're not laughing at you, Des," Mum said, trying to stop her face from crumpling up.

I beat my hands in the pillow. "They are mum they are! You are!"

She tried to hold me and I shook her off. She was quiet for a bit, so quiet I thought she had gone but she was just sitting there. She gave me a bunch of tissues and she might have held me then but there was still a quiver on her face. "I'm sorry ... but come on Des, it is funny -"

"There you are! There you are!" I yelled at her and she left me and I heard them come in, one after another, Grandad, then, as I was dropping asleep, Almost. Mum crept in and I thought it was to kiss me goodnight but she opened my clothes cupboard and put something in and crept out again. She was always putting my school clothes away and I was about to drift off but there was a thud and something rolled across the floor towards me. I stared at the police truncheon. Hanging up was the uniform. I pulled it down, scrunched it up all over again, went blindly through the room into the kitchen. Before I had put in with all the paper waste. This time I buried it with the scrap food and other muck as Mum pulled me away, shouting at me, my truncheon rolling over the floor again.

"Why doesn't he come and join us? Since that's what we're talking about?"

Nobody said "yes" and nobody said "no" but Mum began to be Mum again and put me on her knees with her arms round me and they sort of forgot about me as they began to talk. Almost said Mr Next-Week should have gone up himself and checked. Grandad said some boring stuff about police being understaffed or something. He would ensure there were more police guarding Fourways Tower. That did make my eyes close. Mum got up to take me back to bed. Then Almost said something which made my eyes jerk open and her sit down with a bump.

"It won't happen again." He finished his fish and chips and clattered his knife and fork back on his plate.

"Oh. You know that, do you?" Grandad said. He didn't like Almost much. I once heard him arguing with Mum about him. She said: "He's a car mechanic!" and Grandad said "He's a little bit of this and a little of that."

"It won't happen on this block," Almost said. "They've done this one for a year or so. That's why they've thrown away the Sucker's List."

"Where do you plan to go next?" Grandad said.

Almost stood up, snatching up his plate and what he always used to call his irons. I thought he was going to throw them at Grandad who looked about to duck.

"Dad!" Mum said. "Stop it!"

"Can't you all take a joke?" Grandad said.

"Joke!" Almost muttered. "People thieve because they can't get money any other way."

"How about working?" Grandad said

"That's what I did."

"Stop it, stop it both of you!" Mum said. "Or I'll throw both of you out - won't we Des?"

"Yes Mum, " I said. "With my truncheon!"

Everybody howled with laughter at that and beat the table with their hands, I don't know why.

Mum said what Almost meant was that he picked up gossip from old mates who brought in cars. He wouldn't say no more But one day he picked me up from school and was fastening my seat belt when a van with a big, broken roof rack pulled up. The driver had a lot of tattoos which I thought were terrific, including a sword and shield on the back of one of his hands.

He said something about working on Green Tower and would Almost have a look at his van. Almost shook his head and said he didn't do that sort of job any more. The tattoo-man gave a twiddle with his thumb and fingers which I knew meant money. Almost shook his head all sharp-like and closed my window so I couldn't hear no more. The tattoo-man thumped the roof of our car all angry-like as we drove off.

I asked who he was and Almost said an idiot. Shortly, before we got to our flats, we passed a block called Green Tower. The workmen who had been on our block were now on this one. Almost slowed and stared at the vans parked.

"Is Green Tower where they're going next?" I said.

"Who?"

"The robbers."

Almost braked sharp and swerved, nearly going into a car pulling out. He yelled at the driver, parked near our block and as he unclipped me said cops and robbers wasn't a game. He was glad I'd thrown my uniform away.

"Miss Hancock tells us to report things that are suspicious," I said.

"Does she. Well. That's different. I mean don't go looking for it. Understand?"

I'd thrown my uniform away but not my truncheon. I liked my truncheon. It was on my fave shelf, along with a whistle I had found and a pair of broken binoculaurs through which I could see if any skyscrapers were invading. And, on another day, when Almost picked me up from school and I was supposed to be doing my homework I stared out of the window. Through my binoculaurs I saw in the nearby Green Tower a van with a big, rusty roof-rack hanging down the back.

Almost was going to clear out his van in the yard and I asked Mum if I could go with him.

"Fifteen minutes. Both of you," she said.

I wish I hadn't thrown my uniform away. I was a policeman again. What Almost was doing was boring. I unlocked my bike and rode around. At the back of our block was an entrance which led to what was little more than a bike track which ran by the side of a canal. I was told never to go down there but if I just got to a little bridge, I thought, I could see the Green Tower. It was just out of sight. I crossed the bridge and I could just see it, out of sight in the yard outside the tower: the van with the big rusty roof-rack. They were all built the same, these blocks. There was a desk in the hall where the warden lived, a big friend of Mr Next-Week , Mr Never. I cycled into the car park, skidded into the bottom of the steps and ran up them panting. Mr Never was at his desk, on the phone.

"Thief! ... Thief! ..."

"What? Just a minute," he said to the phone and covered it, looking down at me.

"Thieves," I said. "That van!"

He burst into laughter and said: "You don't fool me, young man."

"The van with a roof ra-"

"He's working here! If you don't stop fooling about I *will* call the police. For *you*!" And he went back on the phone.

It all came back to me when the police had come to our block. The laughter. I remembered it at school, Stewart laughing at me. It would happen all over again. What a fool I was, what an idiot! I went slowly down the steps. A woman was picking up my bike. She told me not to leave it on the steps like that .

I trudged up to the van. *Was* it the same van as I'd seen before? There were lots of vans with battered roof racks. The driver of this was half-asleep, a fag hanging from his mouth. He was not a bit like the man I had seen coming to see Almost. I got on my bike and began to cycle to the canal bridge. I don't know what made me do it but as I reached it I took one last look at Green Tower. Walking down the steps was a man with a tool-bag. I did a circle round before crossing the bridge. The man had arms tattooed with sword and shields I recognised. He was putting a hand-bag in the tool-bag. Even then I didn't mean to, I scarcely knew I was doing it until I heard it - the whistle round my neck I was blowing.

The man stopped. He sort of jumped in the air as if he had been shot. I gave the whistle another long blow. This robber ran towards me, ripped the whistle from me so the string cut into my neck. His fist hit me. The world was full of pain as I hit the grass at the edge of the canal and I could see his boot coming towards me.

It never hit me. A hand caught the boot and twisted it round. Tattoo-man hit the ground near me. And Almost was on top of him and that's all I saw before I passed out.

And I still got told off! Mum went bananas for me going over the canal and as for blowing that whistle ... ! I was in bed for a couple of days. Sergeant Wilcox came to talk to me and Almost about what he called was the assault by Joe Butcher, the tattoo-man.

Almost said he had been working on his car in our yard, couldn't see me and had come looking for me.

"Did you know Joe Butcher?" Sergeant Wilcox asked Almost.

"Never seen him in my life before," Almost said.

Sergeant Wilcox looked at me. "What made you blow the whistle, Des?"

"I saw the van ..." Almost's eyes were still on me. "I saw the man with tattoos putting a handbag in his tool bag and I didn't think men used handbags..."

Everybody laughed at me - but at least they were laughing in the right kind of way.

Broomstick

After that I was a bit of all right with Mrs Grumble. For a bit. When I passed her flat after school she always gave me a biscuit. Mum said I had to take them although they were horrible digestives. I began to creep past but although her door was closed she always seemed to see me.

"PC Des ... Here you are!"

Mum said I had to eat them. They were good for me. Soon I had a drawer full of mouldering digestives. Whenever she opened the door she had a biscuit in one hand and a brush in the other. Once when she saw Mum bringing up a vacuum from repairs she told her she wouldn't waste money on a drycleaner. They didn't suck muck out - they blew it into the carpet.

"Mrs Grumble doesn't brush with it," Grandad said. "She flies on it."

"For God's sake don't give him ideas," Mum said. "You know what he's like."

"Flies on it?" I said.

"It's a broomstick." Grandad pulled back the curtain. It was getting cold and the clouds were like clumps of dark muck over torn-up bits of moon. He pointed. "There she is. See her?"

There was something. Briefly across a strip of moon before it was swallowed up by the black cloud.

"Yes, there is something," Mum said. "Something landing at Heathrow."

Clouds swirled round a plane dipping lower and lower. "Silly Grandad!" I said.

"Maybe," Grandad said. "But I'll bet there's spells in those digestive biscuits."

I had some homework to do. Rotten old sums. My worst subject. I'd make some excuse at school. Forgotten them or something. I started to play football on the telly. Mum gave me a row, pulling out the plug when I wouldn't stop. She wouldn't help me. Grandad said he couldn't add up any more.

"Liar!" I shouted.

"Do not call your Grandad a liar!"

She was really cross. I was crying. She told me I was not going to get my pudding until I had finished my work. She put the maths book on the table in my room and closed the door. I blew my nose with my finger and thumb and threw the snot on the floor and folded my arms. I was not going to do the work ever, ever, *ever*! I was not! That would show her. I heard Almost come in and have his pasta. Then I smelt the pudding. Apple crumble. She did it with custard. Thick custard. I got up and went to the door. Stopped. I knew what she would say. Show me your work. I snatched up my pen. I would scribble anything in. I threw the pen at the window. She would go over them. I went to the door. They were laughing! Laughing! There was the clink of spoons on plates - and I was so hungry!

The drawer from which I had taken my pen was still open. It was full of digestive biscuits. She had given me one that day. It looked as if there were currants in it. I could pick them out.. Yes. Three, big, juicy currants.

I was about to pick them out when I remembered Grandad saying there were spells in it. Grandad was always saying silly things. I knew there were no such things as spells but I still dropped it back in the drawer. It fell currants side up. One was the biggest currant I had ever seen, poking right out of the edge of the biscuit. A drop of saliva trickled from the corner of my mouth. I swallowed, shut the drawer and turned away. Our tower block was an L-shaped building. Mrs Grumble's flat was on the same floor as ours, on the turning of the L.

She had the window open and I could see her, as usual, brush in hand, sweeping. Or was she? Her room was dark except for some light from the corridor. There was a streak of something swallowed up by the clumps of heavy, dark cloud. A flock of birds? The curtain flapped from Mrs Grumble's wide-open window. Come on! I was being as stupid as Grandad! But suppose she was a witch. Just suppose ... I opened the drawer of biscuits. Suppose, suppose there were such things as spells. I had read somewhere that witches granted wishes.

I ate the biscuit and chewed the sweet delicious currant and took a digestive which wasn't too bad with the currants and made a wish.

"Mrs Grumble ... please give me a good mark with the sums ..."

I stared out of the window, half-expecting something. Nothing. Just dark clouds - nothing. It was rubbish. I pulled out the homework. Make each number add up to 30. 10 + ? I scribbled 20. 18 + ? I put 18 + 13 = 30.

There was a rumble of thunder. A shiver went down me. I stared out of the window. It seemed darker. The curtain in Mrs Grumble's window flapped. What made 18 into 30? I counted on my fingers, slowly, painfully. What was the point of adding up in your head when you could do it so much faster by computer? I crossed out 13 and put 18+12= 30. I had never spent so much time doing arithmetic. I heard mum open the door once, then creep away. When I did finish my head was nodding asleep on my desk. She brought me my apple crumble but I couldn't eat it. I had eaten the whole of a drawer of digestive biscuits.

Or was it spells? I got nine out of ten right in my arithmetic. It just shows what you can do if you try Mum said. When I told her about the biscuits all she said was if they helped me pass exams, I should keep eating them. I had none left. But surely spells were what made things just happen! With a snap of the fingers. You didn't have to add up! The spirits did it.

I remembered how Mr Magic waved his hands and ten pound notes appeared in them. He did a kind of waving blur. I tried to remember the way he waved his hands when I next did my arithmetic. I got three out of ten. Magic was rubbish. I tried to stop thinking about it by practicing on football. Mr Hunter was picking his team to play Grangefield Lower. I had spent so much time on magic I had missed a key match and it looked as though Mr Hunter was going to pick Stewart as our key forward. Would I get a place at all?

After missing practice matches Mr Hunter took me to one side to "have a few words."

"Her hem," he started. When I hear that, I always stop listening. "You're a good player, Des ... " When I hear that I always stop listening even more cos I know he's going to say something rotten to me. "... you can be a very good player but er hem ... football is a team game. You can get through on your own but *passing* to others, working with others is what makes a winning team ..."

I felt double-rotten. I couldn't say anything at first when Mum picked me up. The sky was black. The world was black. Eventually when she asked me what was wrong I told her he was going to pick that bastard Steward.

"Don't call him a bastard."

"That bastard Stewart."

She went into the flats. I trailed after her. Mrs Grumble had been away for a week but the lights were now on in her flat.

"Hunter said I was selfish," I said.

"Well ..." Mum said. She gave me one of her her ah hems. "You are a bit, Des... "

I stormed into my room. The whole world was rotten. The whole world hated me. I hated the world! Everyone. It rained. I could see Stewart's face when he read the team Mr Hunter pinned up on the board.

"Bad luck, Des."

Bastard.

I went to bed but couldn't sleep. There was a rumble of thunder. It sounded the same rumble when I thought I had seen Mrs Grumble fly through the sky. Did people's hearts stop? Mine did when I had the worst possible thought that had ever ever come to me: was Hunter going to pick me *at all*? Was he going to leave me out? Is that what he was saying? I could hear that "Her ... Hem" in his voice in another roll of thunder.

I made a wish. Please let him pick me. Please. I didn't feel anything. There was no roll of thunder. Nothing.

The magic wishes didn't work. Only the digestive biscuits worked. I pulled open the drawer. No biscuits. Not a crumb. A currant. There was a swirl of wind, blowing rain against the window. The lights were on in Mrs Grumble's flat. I could just see her television flickering. I left my bedroom. Mum was half-asleep in front of our telly.

"What is it, sweetie?"

"Want a biscuit."

"I'll do you a cocoa."

"One of Mrs Grumble's biscuits."

She half-laughed and hit the chair with her hand. "You can't ask Mrs Grumble for a biscuit! At this time of night. Go on. Take one from the tin."

I went into the kitchen and searched our tin for one of the magic digestives that might have been put in there. Chocolate. Jam sponges. Not one digestive! I wandered out. Mum was watching a thriller. A man with a gun slipping through bushes. Everything in my life seemed to depend on that biscuit. Those magic currants. I crept to our door and opened it. The corridor was empty. I reached up and rang Mrs Grumble's bell. There were sounds of shots being fired. It sounded as though Mrs G was watching the same thriller. I rang the bell again. Twice. I pushed open the letter box. I could see down the hall. Mrs Grumble was at the entrance to one of her rooms.

"Who is it?" she shouted.

"Desmond. Can I have a biscuit?"

Before she could answer Mum was grabbing me away, apologising to Mrs Grumble as she came to the door saying she thought it was one of those thieves again and I could have one of her biscuits if I wanted to but Mum shook her head, shoved me back in our flat and locked the door.

So no biscuit. No magic. And I wasn't picked as centre forward. Stewart was. In some ways I'd rather not have been picked at all when I saw the look on Stewart's face.

"Tough shit, Des," he said.

It was the key match of the year, against Grangehill Lower. And Hunter had put me in *defence*. Not even midfield. Full back! Well, I determined to show him! I was faster than any of our other players. And I was getting really good with my left foot. I would show him. I would streak up the wing and score at my first opportunity.

It was a really scratchy match for most of the first half. Then, in the second half, I got the ball, beat a player and went down the wing. I saw Hunter yelling at me to centre it to Stewart but I ran for goal. I was brought down, flat on my face in the mud. Foster, the Grangefield player who had robbed me went for our goal. Because I was out of position he scored. There was so much mud on my face and in my ears I could scarcely hear what Hunter said to his assistant Beecham but I didn't need to. The expressions on their faces were enough. They were talking about taking me off.

Almost immediately, Stewart ran for goal, jumped, and scored a header. It was good. Even I had to admit it. I had to score. I *must* score! I had to score the winner while I was still on. We were in the last five minutes. I began moving forward again. Grangefield's Foster seemed to sense it, got the ball from me and turned to run through. I tackled him and saw a way through and went for it. I could see the goal.

It was a long shot but I was sure I could get it. Right in the corner. The crowd were yelling. I drew back my foot. Then I saw Stewart running towards the centre. I hesitated. Foster was coming through to tackle me. I centred. As soon as I'd kicked it I was sure I'd got it wrong. It was too close to the goal. Their goalie was jumping for it. But Stewart leapt forward, his head getting there first and the ball was in the net.

Even I had to admit it was a fantastic goal. Everybody was around Stewart, clapping his back. The whole crowd. I was alone when I trudged back into the dressing room. Then I felt someone coming up behind me. A hand touched my shoulder. It was Mr Hunter.

"Great pass, Des," he said. That's what wins matches."

Flying Machines

I didn't know what "rebuild" meant. What happened in this story taught me.

Mr Next-Week now saluted me when I came in. He no longer saw me as someone who nicks things - a banana from his desk in the hall - but as the boy who caught a robber. He even allowed me to chain my bike to the railings once. That didn't last long. Leaflets from *Rebuild*, the campaign by people who lived in the tower blocks to make them safer, used to come. Mr Next Week used to bin them. I used to turn them into flying machines and chuck them out of my bedroom window with Almost to see who could fly them furthest.

I'd stopped having bad dreams. I'd stopped even seeing Grenfell. It was there as if it had always been there. A black tower. The only time I had a dim memory of what had happened was when Almost took me for a pizza at his local, *Next Please*. Jimmy, a builder Almost knew, said companies were being asked how much it would cost to work on our tower.

Almost told me what scaffolding was and said Jimmy might be walking past my window to say goodnight. I liked Almost meeting Jimmy because each felt he had to buy the other a drink and I got an extra coke out of it. We were late back and Mum was still in her uniform and in a rotten mood. I wanted to play football on the telly and she wouldn't let me.

"I've been on a twelve-hour shift," she said to Almost. "And I thought he would be in bed at least."

He'd stopped at the shop to get some fags and bought a little bottle of white wine Mum liked and I got a bag of crisps out of that one.

He gave her the white wine. She turned it round and round in her hand, said thank-you, but not right now thank-you, let's just get him to bed, shall we, and she told me to get my jamas on but she steered him into a corner of the room and said something, I don't know what, but they began having an argument. I wandered about the room ... then I saw it! Not just one *Rebuild* leaflet - a whole packet! They made excellent flying machines. I would have a fly-the-furthest with Almost.

I was just bending and smoothing the wings on a Super-Fly to beat Almost when Mum cried: "Leave that!"

I stared at her, still smoothing out the wings, like I'd done with leaflets before, or chucked them in the rubbish. She snatched it from me. It tore, one of the best Super-Flys I'd ever made. She shouted "I said leave them! ... I told you to put your pyjamas on!"

I began to cry. Almost steered me towards my bedroom. "Ok, ok Des, your Mum's had a very long day and she's very upset - "

"Of course I'm upset! Aren't you upset? I told you what would happen didn't I?"

"All right, all right, I'll just, just - "

He chucked my pyjamas at me and went back to her. "I've just seen Jimmy-"

"At *NextPlease*. I'll bet you have."

"They're in the running for the job here and -"

"Have you read this leaflet?"

I got my things on. I could hear them arguing. No-one to read me a story. No telly. No Super-Fly. No nothing. I was about to fling myself on the bed when I saw something strange through the window. I never saw the black tower of Grenfell when it was night but I saw it now. It was burning. Burning all over again.

"Mum! Mum! It's burning!"

"What? Where?" She rushed into my room. "What are you talking about?"

I pointed out of the window. "Oh Des, Des!" She held me and hugged me. "You scared me to death! I thought ... I thought we were ..."

She opened the window and held me up so I could see properly. There were red lights and flames but they were candles burning, held by a crowd of people. Two of them held a banner which said: **REBUILD NOW!**

She tucked me into bed and told me a story until I was half asleep but I couldn't get to sleep cos they were arguing so loud.

"You haven't been listening to a word I said, have you? They're not going to do *any* rebuilding!"

"Several companies have been asked to quote for it."

"Now they've seen the size of the bill, the company that owns the freehold of this dump want leaseholders like us to pay part of it".

"What? We can't afford that! Nobody can!"

I hadn't understood a word of this but I understood what Mum said next.

"Right. So what do you want? Us to become Grenfell Two?"

It was funny. Strange. The funniest fireworks night I'd ever been to. They were bangers. Bangers going off. But they weren't making any noise. Silent bangers exploding in the sky. It was a bangers party I once went to with my mate Tom at the park near the school. But there was no fire. Just smoke. And it wasn't in the park. We were in the flat. And we were racing upstairs but it wasn't racing upstairs like we once tried to do, we were fighting to get downstairs. There was the lift but the lift wasn't working and Tom wasn't there, I was trying to reach him, but he wasn't there, I was fighting for brea ... brea ...

"All right ... darling ..."

I was burning hot, I was frightened of someone screaming and then I realised it was me. I was wet, everything was wet and mum gave me something and walked me round the flat round and round until I fell asleep.

I didn't go to school next day. I was with mum all day. I liked that. After three twelve hour shifts she had four days and said she was like a real mum.

"I want a real dad," I said.

"Never mind that," she said.

"What were you dreaming about?" the doctor asked.

"Bonfire night," I said.

"It wasn't bonfire night, was it?"

"Mine was."

They talked about tablets and boring things liked that and he scribbled something on a piece of paper which Miss Hancock would have given him no marks for. He was a funny old man with not much hair and big glasses. When mum was at the door he said: "Tell him."

While we were walking through the waiting room I said: "Tell him ... tell me what?"

She shook her head. I felt better. It was great. It was one of her real mum days and I was off school and we were going to go to the pictures! But then she said she had to go to a meeting.

"You *said* we could go! You promised! You *said* you weren't working!"

"I'm not. I'm sorry but ... this isn't work it's ... listen Des ... listen ..."

She told me to listen but then said nothing for me to listen to. I kicked a stone and she told me to stop kicking stones so I kicked one harder and hurt myself and she dragged me along to this meeting where she said there was a play area. There was. For toddlers. Bricks and a toy house. There was only one thing I could play with. A packet of those *Rebuild* leaflets. There was another kid Gareth there. I showed him how to build a Super-Fly and although we were only two floors up there was a garage roof that made a great landing area and I was winning four-three when Mum came out of the meeting. With her was a mum I knew I knew but couldn't remember her name at first.

"It's Amy love ..." Mum said. "Tom's mum ... Tom who ... who ..."

"Who died in the fire," Amy said.

"He scored," I said. "Tom was our scorer."

"He did. You passed and - he ... he ... " She held me and hugged me.

"He was good."

"He was ... he was, Des ... Will you help us? ... Deliver leaflets and things...?"

"Course ... course I will ... leaflets ... course ... leaf ..."

Is the Patient Breathing?

I never made another of those Super-Flys. But I delivered a ton of those leaflets. I cycled around with Mum or Amy. Sometimes Grandad took me in his car to deliver them round Forest Park. You had to go down a long, twisty, smelly concrete underpass to get from the estate to Forest Park. The leaflets took me into a different world. There weren't no forest and not much of a park but there were gardens like what I'd never seen before. When I asked Grandad who lived there he said robbers.

"Or should I say worked here." He pointed to a metal sign WATCH which glittered on the wall just below the roof. "So did we when I was in the police."

He delivered to about two houses while I ran and did the rest of the street.

"You must close the gates here Des," he said.

"Why?"

He was breathing heavy. "Just do it will you."

I was getting fed up of leaflets and fed up of Grandad. When I opened the packet he told me to pick up the plastic wrapper and walk half-way down the street to the litter bin. You never picked things up in Fourways Tower. There weren't no bins or they were full or collapsing or rusted.

The biggest and best street was Chestnut Grove. It overlooked the park. It was after school and football and I was a bit nackered and I went in through the side-gate and across the grass. A rapping at the window made me jump. A witch with scrawny white hair and black glasses was waving me away with crooked fingers. I had one leaflet which, bored in the car, I had made into a Super-Fly. I bombed it into The Witch's porch and ran back to the sidegate - straight into Grandad who was waiting there.

He gave me his policeman look. "That wasn't very clever."

The Witch came down the path, her arms folded. "Is he yours?"

"Yes madam."

He shook me and told me to say sorry to the lady. First she was *madam* and now she was *lady*. They even talked different here. I mumbled sorry.

He gave me a shove. "Properly!"

I told her I was sorry again and he told her we were Rebuild, and then what Rebuild was, with smile after smile, and he looked over trees and pointed. I could see several grey smudges, tower blocks which included Fourways. Then he told me to walk up the "proper" path and give the lady the "proper" leaflet - everything had to be proper here - and pick up my rubbish.

Rubbish! My Sky-Fly wasn't *rubbish*! It had landed perfectly in the Witch's porch. I hated Grandad and was never going to speak to him again or deliver one of those stinking leaflets.

In the car, Grandad looked about to turn the key to start but didn't. He put his hand on my shoulder, but it wasn't a "do this" movement. He gave me a squeeze.

"I'm sorry Des," he said. "I know you think I'm a pain ... but ... but if you want to get on in this life you have to be nice to people like that."

"Why?"

"Why? Why? Why? Yes … well …" He scratched his head. "That's a very good question. Because we have to try and get them to give us money so we can persuade the government to rebuild them."

He pointed to the grey smudges over the trees.

"Why?"

"Why? That's an even better question!" He laughed. He laughed so much I began to laugh with him, although I had no idea what we were laughing about.

When Mum was on shift I was taken around by Almost, although he said it was a load of rubbish and would never get us anywhere. I began to think he was right when the dark nights came and I even got fed-up with the dodge-the-wardens game.

One rainy night Almost picked me up after school. Mum was working at the hospital. He took me for a pizza before picking up a pack of leaflets and other stuff. The rain really came down and Almost parked right outside the glass front doors of the tower. Mr Next-Week saw us and waved us away. As Almost was unloading the *Rebuild* package and other things he came out, umbrella up.

"You can't park there!"

"I'm only bringing the kid in!" Almost said.

"Double yellow!"

There was a rumble. A bang. I thought it was thunder. Almost waved me to come. I jumped out of the car. I tripped and almost fell. Mr Next-Week was yelling something. Almost had stopped and was looking up towards the top of the tower. I started to run towards the door but Almost grabbed me and dragged me back.

Mr Next-Week was coming towards us, shouting something. Almost shouted back at him. Something hit me. A small stone. A much bigger stone, a sort of panel hit Mr Next-Week. Another. There were clouds of dust amongst the pouring rain.

"Keep back," yelled Almost. "Back back back in the car!"

I scrambled back in the car. Mr Next-Week's legs were bending one way then another. He fell all slow-like. I couldn't see him. I couldn't see anyone. The car was shaking. Almost was shaking me.

"Des ... Are you ok? Des ... Des ..."

I sicked up my food. He got some tissues and wiped my face..

"Des ... say something ..."

"W ... want Mum."

"Yeh, ok kid, we'll get Mum. Just a minute .... I must just ..."

He ran through the rain which had cleared the dust and I could see the huddled lump of Mr Next-Week. Almost took off his coat and put it over him and came back to the car. I could hear a bit of the phone answer.

"Ambulance emergency ... is the patient breathing?"

"Yes, yes ... Fourways Tower ... he's been hit on the head by falling bricks ... panels from a tower block ... and there's an eight year old, I think he's ok, but ... but ..."

"We've had a call from upstairs ... There are already two ambulances on the way ..."

Near Mr Next-Week was a packet of *Rebuild* leaflets and posters getting soaked in the rain. I ran out of the car.

"Get back in the car!" Almost shouted.

"Mum wouldn't like - "

"*Get back!*"

I chucked the packet through the open door of the car, slipped and fell in against the seat, feeling dizzy, pulling myself in. People were running down the stairs and coming out of the lift into the hall, pushing towards the door, some carrying things they had grabbed, some with coats over their heads, staring up at the top of the tower, as if afraid that more blocks were going to fall. One of them was Mrs Grumble, her voice sharp among the running feet and shouting.

"Does Mr Bottomley know about this?"

It was a bit before I knew she meant Mr Next-Week. She walked and spoke as if she thought he could do something about it.

"This is Mr Bottomley," Almost said. "Another coat someone."

Someone was telling Almost not to move him, but he was partly up, half his face a sheet of blood, the eye I could see closed before the tower seemed to swing to one side and then to the other and there was the sound of the siren in the distance as I fell back against the seat.

I wanted to be in an ambulance going in a dee-dor-dee-dor-dee-dor at top speed with traffic getting out of my way but I was in one going at no miles an hour. They gave me something that put me into a long sleep. When I woke up I thought the nurse was mum at first because she had mum's uniform on. She got mum.

"I got the leaflets, mum," I said.

"Yes ... you what ... you got ..." She had tears in her eyes and held me and kissed me. "You ... you ... you got the leaflets ..." She couldn't hold me properly because I had bandages on my head and left hand.

"Is my head broke?"

"No darling, no .... You have concussion."

"Con - cushion?"

"Something like that."

"What happened to Mr Next-Week?"

"Don't call him that."

He nearly wasn't Any-Week. I saw him once when I was leaving hospital. He had one eye and the rest of his face was bandaged. He was in a wheelchair. I learned what happened to him one night when Almost collected me from school and took me for a pizza at the *NextPlease*. We were eating out more often because while people were talking about mending the broken bits of Fourways we were living with Grandad.

Jimmy the builder bought everything, even my pizza and coke.

"We got it!" he said. He and Almost raised their glasses. I raised mine in the hope they would buy me another coke.

"We got it." Jimmy said. "Even though we were far from being the cheapest."

"How did that happen?" Almost said.

"We're the safest," Jimmy said. "And the owners paid up when they found out what the solicitors got for the poor bloody warden who will never walk again and three others injured."

"What's a ... soli - ci - tor?" I asked.

"Someone who makes money from mistakes," Almost said.

"Can I make mistakes?" I said.

They howled with laughter, thumped the table and Jimmy bought me another coke.

Suspects

"Never mind West Tower falling down," Almost muttered. "Ivy Cottage looks as though it's already fallen down."

Ivy Cottage was where Grandad lived. He said the estate agents had sold it to him for his retirement as a period dwelling. "Period what?" said Almost. "In Yorkshire we'd call it a two up and two down."

"You should be grateful we've got anywhere!" snapped Mum.

"I am I am! He just won't let me do anything!"

Grandad lived down and we lived up. I couldn't see no ivy but the slide was terrific. It was the polished banister rail and I helped to polish it by sliding down, jumping at the bottom on to the mat by the front door. It got more and more wobbly until one day there was a crack and it jerked loose and I went sailing through the air, hitting the door with a crash. Everything spun about me. Grandad shouted, clutching the drooping rail.

"Leave him!" Mum cried. "He's hurt!"

"*He's* hurt! What about my rail?" Grandad cried.

"I'll fix it," Almost said. He said you always had to be on the job these days, ready at a moment's notice to fix anything. His dungarees were nearly all pockets and held all his tools. While I was still in a daze he had a spanner and a chisel out.

"I'll fix it." Grandad said.

"You can't leave it like that!" Almost said.

"I said I'll fix it!" Grandad shouted. He took the rail from Almost. He didn't say anything for a bit and then he said in a quieter voice: "I prefer to do things my own way, thank you."

I was out of the daze. I was crying for a bit but I think it was cos of the shouting more than the hurt but Mum looked at the bit of my head that the tile hurt and put me back to bed. I didn't want to go to bed. I couldn't do my homework. I had got a good mark last time, answering the question: "What does it mean to be brave?"

I had written about how Almost had rescued Mr Next-Week. This question was:

"What was the best thing about today and what was the worst?" I wrote 'best and worst' were the same. The slide. Grandad fixed it but he didn't fix it. It was wonkier than ever. I used to like going to Grandad's but I hated it now. You musn't do this and you musn't do that. Knock before you go into the toilet. Grandad seemed to sleep on it.

There was what Almost called the police wall. There were pictures of Grandad in uniform, one of an award and another of a newspaper cutting with a picture of him and the headline: **Detective Arrests Killer.**

"Will he arrest me?" I said.

"He will if you don't behave yourself."

Sometimes it was funny. Sometimes it wasn't. One morning I put a leg over the banister. Just a leg, that was all, but everything creaked and cracked in that place and Mum shot out of our room and yanked me off.

"Do *not* use that as a slide!"

"I wasn't. I was testing it."

"God give me strength. If you don't stop doing that Desmond Taylor we'll have to leave."

"Why?"

Her face was red. She was shaking. "Why why why why why!" she shouted. "I am fed up with being asked why, Mr Why - just *do* it, right?"

Almost stuck his head out of our room. "Let me fix it," he whispered. "It's a bit dangerous as it is."

"You touch that bloody slide I mean banisters and we are *out*. We will have to leave. L-e-a-v-e! Don't either of you understand?"

"All right all right," Almost said. "There's no need to go mental."

"Mental? Mental am I? - "

There was a small rumble of thunder and a rush of water as the toilet flushed. Grandad came out whistling, humming and singing. "... She loves you... yeah yeah yeah ..."

Before we'd come to Ivy Cottage I'd never heard of The Beatles. There you heard bits of them every other minute. Grandad was always singing about love but nobody seemed to love one another at Ivy Cottage. He looked upstairs. He didn't seem to have heard any of the shouting. "Anyone seen my hearing aids?"

"In your ear?" Mum said.

"What?"

"*In your ear!*" she yelled.

"There's no need to shout," he said, feeling in his ears. "Oh yes. I mean batteries ... With a love like that you know it can't be bad ... Has anyone seen my batteries?"

There was nowhere to play, no park near and the narrow, winding street was a cut-through for vans and lorries. Someone had chalked a goal on a wall at the end where Almost and I played football until a lorry almost knocked me over and that was a no-no.

The cellar was a no-no until the day Grandad couldn't find his batteries. It was a spooky, mysterious hole under the stairs, with shaky wooden steps. Mum said a ghost lived down there, but I knew she said that just to keep me out. It was half-term the day it happened. She and Almost had to go to work and Grandad was left to take care of me. She seemed more worried about Grandad than me.

"Have you taken your pills?" she said. "Don't leave them where Des can pick them up ... Amy will pick him up for football at ... Did you hear me?"

"What? ..."

In the end she wrote a note in large capitals and gave it to me and gave me a big hug and said for God's sake find his batteries will you until I felt I was looking after Grandad, not him me. The house felt suddenly empty. He had an old TV and he couldn't find Netflix so I could watch one of my programmes. He wandered round the house, opening drawers, looking on shelves, half-singing, half-muttering ... Yesterday ... Love was such an easy game to play ... I know I put the bloody things somewhere! Someone must have moved them! Why do people touch things! ... Now I need a place to hide away - Oh ... I believe in yester .... day"

"I know!" He struck his hand on the wall so that pictures rattled and one nearly fell off. "The cellar! I remember! I left them with my pills down there so no-one could touch them and I could keep them safe!"

He opened the cellar door and switched on the light. It shone on the rickety wooden stairs. He had his slippers on. He stretched one wavering foot on to the first stair. There was no rail to hang on to and his hand scrabbled on the wall, dislodging little bits of plaster before he grabbed the light switch to hang on to. He mumbled "Oh I believe in yester ..." as he stretched out his other foot for the next step down. The heel of the slipper came away from his foot. He struggled to flip the slipper back on but it dropped into the cellar. He wavered on the stairs, nails scratching the plaster as he fell. For a moment it looked as if he was going to go into the cellar, but he found the edge of the door and I just managed to dodge away as he fell back into the hall, his head banging against the wall.

"Are you all right? ... Grandad?"

He was in a crumpled heap and his eyes were closed. I picked up his iPhone which had fallen from his pocket. "I'll phone Mum."

"What?" His eyes jerked open. "No ... no ... I'm ... I'm ok but ... but I can't get up without support." He pointed towards the kitchen. "That chair."

It was a chair round the breakfast table. It was too heavy for me to lift but I managed to slide it from the kitchen to the hall. He used it to turn himself on to his hands and knees, then pulled himself up and sat heavily on it.

"Stupid ... stupid place to put them! Pills *and* batteries. ... Can you get them, Des?"

I stared down into the cellar. There was as much light as a candle. Mum had said there were ghosts down there. I was no longer so sure she was just saying that to keep me out. It was an old, old house. Looking down those rickety steps at the bare brick walls, at the piles of dirty, dusty boxes, at the dark corners I heard a shuffling sound. A mouse, a rat or ...

"Mum says it's a no-no."

"A what?"

"A no-no!" I shouted.

He slumped back in the chair. "I've got to have those pills ... You can have one of those chocolate biscuits you like."

"Two." I said.

"You little! ... Go on."

I went down the first two steps then turned. The light got dimmer as I went on. There were cobwebs. A spider. Something glinted. In the darkest corner of the cellar something or someone was staring at me. I didn't care how many chocolate biscuits he gave me I was not going down there. I turned to scramble back up. I slipped, grabbed at nothing and fell, hitting a pile of boxes.. I lay on the stone floor, dazed.

"Are you all right?" Grandad shouted.

As I pushed myself up I saw a box on top of the pile slipping and just managed to roll away before it fell, papers and photographs spilling out from it.

"Des?"

Another box was falling. I scrambled away. Someone or something was staring at me. I screamed.

"Des?"

I realised it was me. Me screaming at myself. There was a mirror propped against the wall in the darkest part of the cellar. It was blotched and chipped so that my reflection broke up, shivering into the ghost. I jumped about, sticking out my tongue and making funny, ghost-like faces at myself.

"Are you all right?" Grandad said.

"There is a ghost ... Look Grandad!"

I dragged the mirror in sight of the stairs. By breathing on it I could make even more horrible shapes.

"Pills! Batteries!" he shouted.

Suddenly the cellar was a magical mystery tour. There were dolls which had been Mum's when she was a little girl, next to a shelf which he had cleared for packets of pills and batteries. I got them and the slipper he had dropped and passed them up to him and began to stuff back papers into boxes.

They were boring old police reports and files until I came across a clump of photographs. One was of Almost.

He stared at me. It was Almost and it wasn't. His head was shaven. One picture was of him staring, another side-face. On the back of each picture was: *Stephen Nesbitt. Suspect in case AX350.* There was another picture of a man with a funny look, as if he was about to laugh, which I thought I had seen before. On the back was: *Phillip Johnson AKA Mr Magic. Suspect in case AX350.*

There was a third photograph of a man I hadn't seen before. His hair was cropped. He had a small beard and a smile which made you want to smile back. I just turned it over to read *Robert Taylor* ... when Grandad shouted.

"Des ... what are you doing down there? Don't you want your chocolate biscuits?"

"What's ... Sus ... Sus ...Pect mean?"

"What?"

I shouted: "Sus ... Pect ...!"

"What have you got down there?" His slippers appeared at the top of the steps. He said **** which

Miss Hancock says I can't use. He started to come down then grabbed at the wall and said **** again and then, in a very sharp, not-at-all Grandad voice:

"Put that stuff away! Do you hear me? Come on!"

I dropped the photographs back in the box and was about to pick up other papers when he shouted at me to leave everything and snapped out the light so all I could see was the stairs going up.

I munched the chocolate biscuits and nicked another bit from the tin and asked him again what suspect meant.

"It ... er means ... I suspect ... believe ... think that Desmond Taylor has stolen a third biscuit from the tin."

"It was just a bit - that's all!"

He pointed his finger at me and wagged it. "You're under arrest!"

He was back to being silly Grandad again, got Netflix working, put some pizza on for lunch, then fell asleep. I tried to find Fantasy Football on the telly, lost it and asked Grandad to do it. He groaned. A bubble of spit grew on his mouth, burst and dribbled down his chin. I kicked a squashed football. Grandad gave a long sigh and an even longer snore. I wandered into the hall and opened the cellar door.

My name was Desmond Taylor. The man with a beard and a nice smile was Taylor. Robert Taylor.

I was the only boy in my class without a dad. I wondered. I wondered. Sometimes I felt like the only boy in the world without a dad. No. Everyone had a dad somewhere, whether he knew him or not. I opened the cellar door, switched on the light, crept downstairs and found the picture of Robert Taylor. There was a file near it. It was too dim to read anything. I got upstairs where the light was strong enough to see and opened the file.

"Des ..." Grandad called.

I jumped, started to go downstairs to dump the file, but it slipped from my hands and tumbled into the cellar.

"Des ... Where are you?"

I heard him get up, groan and glimpsed him leaving the front room before I pushed the cellar door shut. Through the gap at the edge of the door I saw him stumble past into the kitchen.

I switched off the light, shut the door and shot upstairs. I was still clutching the picture.

"Des?" he shouted.

I shoved the picture under my bedroom pillow and went to the top of the stairs.

"There you are! Would you like to go to the pictures? See the Lion King?"

Would I like to! Everything else was forgotten! Stewart had seen it of course. Rotten old Stewart had seen every picture in the world! Simba had a dad - King Mufasa. And a rotten enemy like Stewart, Scar. Did I want to see the Lion King?! I think Grandad wanted to see it as well. We had a great afternoon with ice-cream and crisps and cheering on Simba to win his battles over the plains of Africa.

I was Simba and Grandad Scar when we played Snakes and Ladders until Mum came back from work and ran the bath. I'd just got to a ladder to the last bit when she shouted to me to come up.

"I know that tone of voice, Simba," Grandad said and sent me upstairs. Mum wouldn't let me play in the bath. Grandad had bought me a Lion King story but she wouldn't read it.

"Where did you get this?" she said.

She held up the photograph of Robert Taylor. I had become so excited about Lion King I had forgotten all about putting it under my pillow.

"Where did you get this?"

"The cellar." I told her about knocking the boxes over and everything. "Is he my dad?"

She opened her mouth but then turned to the window. It was dark and there was nothing to see but still she just stood there. She stood for such a long time I got out and touched her.

"I also saw a picture of Almost. What's a sus .... pect?"

She told me to get back to bed. "A suspect is someone the police think has done something wrong. Almost was found not guilty."

"What did they think he had done?"

"Repair cars that were used to rob people. He hadn't. He didn't know what they were being used for."

"Where's my dad?"

"I don't know and I don't want to know." She went to the window and stared at nothing again.

"Is he in prison?"

She sat down on the bed and hugged me and kissed me. "He went to prison. I don't know where he is now ... Look Des ... I know you think this is one of your stories but this isn't ... a story. Well, it is, but it's a very nasty story. I know you want see your dad ... but he doesn't want to see you ..."

She brought out her iPhone and found another Lion King story about the threat of scorpions but I wasn't interested in scorpions.

As she turned down the light I said: "What did he do?"

"Mufasa?"

"My Dad!"

"Go to sleep!"

I hated To Be Continued stories. They didn't send me to sleep. They kept me awake. Very awake! I had a dad! He had a nice smile. Why didn't he want to see me? What had he been sent to prison for? Where was he? The story was still being continued downstairs. I could hear Mum and Grandad's voices getting louder and louder. I crept half-way down the stairs. Through the banisters I could see Grandad in his big highbacked chair in the kitchen. Mum was pacing round and round and round.

"Almost was found not guilty," Mum said.

"Yes." Grandad said.

"Why won't you accept that?"

Grandad shrugged. "The court's are not always right."

Mum picked up a milk bottle. For a moment I thought she was going to throw it at Grandad. Then she tipped it in her tea. Some splashed over the table.

"Mike says he's the best car mechanic he's got."

"He is a good car mechanic."

"You're not supposed to have those papers are you?"

"They're copies ... Almost knew what was going on ... what those cars were used for -"

Mum hit the table with her fist. "He wasn't a member of the bloody gang dad! ... He had a difficult upbringing and we ... we get on and -"

"You'll wake Des up!"

I saw her coming out of the kitchen and ran back to bed and when she came into my room I pretended to be asleep.

When Grandad was looking after me one day, and outside cleaning the car, I shot down into the cellar. Everything was neat and tidy. It looked like Mum. The boxes in which I had seen the police photographs had gone.

I hate stories that are unfinished. I hate them. I will not give this story to Miss Hancock. Not until it is finished. That day, in the cellar, I locked my little fingers together and promised myself that some day, some-where, somehow, I would find him. I would find my Dad.

Going, going ...

Mum shook me. "Come on." It was scarcely light. I rolled over and started to fall asleep again. She half-pulled me out of bed and told me to pack my rucksack. As I staggered out of my room I saw Almost leaving. Mum was packing a suitcase on her bed. Almost was throwing clothes from a drawer.

"Where we going?"

"Home. To the flats. Your breakfast is on the table. Rucksack."

Grownups never tell you anything, then expect you to know everything. Grandad came out of his bedroom, his pyjama trousers slipping round his ankles and looked as bewildered as I did. He asked Almost what was going on. Almost didn't hear or didn't want to hear as he went down the stairs, car keys in his mouth, suitcase in his hand. Since I had found those photos they never spoke except for "pass the salt." Grandad screwed his hearing aids in and asked Mum what was happening.

"We're leaving," she said, shutting one suitcase and opening another. "Going back to the flats. Thank you very much for having us."

"Is the roof safe?"

"It's ok dad."

"Is it safe?"

"People have started moving back. Some never left -"

"*Is it -*"

Mum turned to me and told me to go downstairs and have my cereal. I dunno what happened then. I heard them shouting but whenever I appeared they stopped. The house was dead quiet apart from things being chucked into boxes and suitcases. Mum threw my rucksack at me. I packed it and put the telly on to play footer. Mum switched it off.

"It's Grandad's," she said.

"He let's me play!"

"We *are leaving, Desmond Taylor* - do you not understand anything!"

I switched the telly on again. She was horrible to me and switched it off and I screamed and shouted and looked for Grandad who was in the street emptying the boot of his car. I asked him if I could play my football but he took no notice of me, no-one was taking any single notice of me at all. Almost was parking a van. Grandad walked up to him. Almost clenched his fists as he approached and I was sure he was going to bash him one.

"I'll take some stuff if you insist on going," Grandad said.

"We're ok. Thanks," Almost said and walked into the house.

Grandad followed him for a few steps and it looked as though he was going to bash him one and all. I was about to ask him again if I could play footer on his telly but this looked more interesting. Grandad slammed the boot of his car a terrific crash, opened the driving door, then came round and gave me a hug.

"Look after them, Des."

Look after them? I don't know what he meant. What anything meant. As he walked back the sun came out. It glinted in the front tyre of the car. Glint? Rubber didn't glint. I bent and thought I saw a bit of nail. When Almost picked me up from school we sometimes went back to the garage where he had to finish a job and I had seen him check tyres. I shouted to Grandad but he was starting the car and didn't hear me. The car didn't start properly. I shouted to Almost who was coming out with Mum, carrying cases.

"What is it Des?" Almost said.

"Is that a nail?"

As Almost dropped his case and bent to look at the tyre Grandad's car roared into life and he began to drive off. Grandad had to stop for an approaching car and Almost hammered at his window. Grandad wound down his window.

"That tyre needs seeing to," Almost said.

"Thanks," Grandad said, and started to put up the window.

"Stop!" shouted Almost, shoving his hand in to stop the window closing. "The engine light's flashing."

"I'm taking it in for service."

"Do you want me to look at it?"

"No thanks." Grandad wound up the window and he began to edge out as the approaching car passed.

"What's wrong?" Mum asked.

Almost shrugged. "Some engine fault. I wouldn't drive in that car but he won't listen."

Mum stepped into the road as Grandad pulled out. He screeched to a stop, his bumper touching her jeans.

"If that light's flashing even I know you shouldn't drive it."

"It's early warning. I'm taking it in for service."

"Dad ... please let him see it."

He gave Mum his Police Inspector look squared. "Jess ... will you please move out of my way!"

She did, but as he started to move again, wrenched open his door. "You worry about us going back to a place with a roof they're still fixing but you won't let him take up the bonnet for five minutes!"

Grandad shut his eyes, muttered something, and released the bonnet. Almost got his tool-bag, looked at the engine, then crawled under the car.

"It's the converter," he said.

"What's a converter?" I asked.

"Bit after this," Almost said, touching the exhaust pipe. "Turns the muck that comes from the engine into less muck."

"I'll take it straight in." Grandad said.

"You can't drive this!" Almost said. "They'll have to tow it in."

"Can you do it?" Mum said.

Almost shook his head. "Not if we're gonna move."

He put a suitcase in the back of the van. While we finished loading the van Grandad rang his garage and then another one. By the time we were ready to go he looked really fed up and said he couldn't find anyone to do it. There was a long argument between Mum and Almost which ended with Almost saying that it was too long a job if they were going to leave that day.

"I'll help you," I said.

Almost gave one of his grunts and said: "Oh ... well ... that's different then, innit."

Everybody started laughing, I don't know why. Almost got stuff from the garage and worked on the car. Mum unpacked food and did sandwiches and I held things until I got bored with it and asked Grandad if

I could do footer on the telly and he said: "Course you can."

I've never done so much footer and through the window I saw Almost turn lights on on the car and Grandad helped him while Almost, who had never ever talked with Grandad proper said things about his car and things that had been packed were gradually un-packed including my pyjamas. Mum hugged me as I went to bed in the cottage and the car was finished but for some reason we were not leaving now and Almost gave me one of his grunts and Grandad said thanks Des and I didn't know what he was thanking me for but it felt all right as I fell asleep.

Grown-ups are funny.

Big Mouth

So we stayed at Grandad's until the roof was fixed. The day we went back to the flats was rotten. It rained. I got my sums all wrong. Miss Hancock snapped. Stewart scored twice against me in football. Mum snapped when she picked me up from school.

"Hat?"

"Haven't got no hat."

"It was on your head this morning Desmond Taylor."

I ran to the cloakroom. My hat was hanging on a hook. I was about to get it when I heard a funny choking sound. Miss Hancock came out of the room next door. She didn't see me because she was on the phone.

"You don't understand ... I don't want to see you ..." She dragged out a crumple of tissues from the sleeve of her jumper and blew her nose. "Because ... because - "

She gulped and wiped a tear from her cheek. People like Miss Hancock don't cry. Teachers know everything and do everything and don't cry. It's only kids like me what cries.

"I know ... I know, you say you love me Gerry but -"

She gulped and a tear trickled down her face. She turned her back and went for some fresh tissues. I crept up to the hook, snatched my hat and had almost sneaked back in the corridor when she called out my name.

"Desmond! Is that you?"

I don't know how it happened but when I turned round she was Miss Hancock again. No sign of tissues, no tears, no crying, no nothing. She snapped at me for forgetting my hat and took me back to mum. Mum must have seen something though, because as we trudged through the rain she asked what was up with her.

"What's love?" I asked.

"Oh. That's the problem," she said and said no more.

"Love?" said Almost, "is what makes the world go round. Or doesn't." and put his head back under the bonnet of the car he was working on.

"Love!" I shouted to Grandad.

"Can you see my hearing aids?" he said.

Mum pointed to them on a table by his chair. "There." she shouted. "Where you were just changing your batteries!"

He winced in pain as he put one aid in. "No need to shout at me. I'm not deaf." He turned to me. "Love," he said.

You never know where you are with Grandad - what he hears and what he doesn't. "I thought you couldn't hear nothing without your aids," I said.

"I can't, Des. But there are a few words you can always lip read."

"What's lip read?"

He gave a long, deep sigh. "Don't you teach this boy anything, Jess?"

"I haven't your experience, dad."

"Your lips become the shape of the word," Grandad said. "You *see* the word instead of hearing it."

His lips came out like a kiss. I clapped my hands. "You mean love is like a kiss!"

"That's it Des! Exactly."

Unlike mum and Almost and Grandma who is dead Grandad listens to children. He gripped my arm as I told him about going back for my hat. His eyes stared and went moist when I told him about Miss Hancock crying.

"Well of course," he said, "teachers *don't* cry. They're teachers. Only children cry. What did she say? When she was crying?"

"I don't know."

"You don't know! Come on Des! You know what Miss Hancock told you about a story."

"It always has a dilemma, a climax and a conclusion," I said miserably. "This only has a dilemma. Her tears."

"I know she *cried*. But what did she *say*!"

Grandad cracked his knuckles while he was trying to remember something. Oddly it helped the words come back to me.

"It was about seeing him. He asked her out."

"Who?"

"Gerry Hunter."

"One of the other teachers," said mum, suddenly joining in. "Music teacher, cropped hair, shadow of a beard, skinny trousers, fancies the world of himself, used to take Miss Hancock out then dropped her for Sophie, head teacher's secretary. Now he's gone off Sophie and trying to get off with Miss Hancock again."

"Rotten at football," I said.

"Mr Hunter won't pick Des for a striker," mum said.

He *was* rotten I thought. He picked Stewart for a striker all because his dad drove a big car. It was the junior football teacher, Mr Burgess, the new maths teacher who wanted to pick me.

"There *is* a new teacher ... Mr Burgess ..." mum said. "The way he keeps looking at Miss Hancock, I'm sure they were going to go out together but he won't say boo-to-a-goose. Now Mr Hunter's back, that could be the finish of it for poor Mr Burgess."

"What's boo-to-a-goose?" I said.

They played their grown-up game of never-u-mind-u-dont-understand. Even Grandad. The next time we had football I was awful. I was midfield and Ginger from Class 3 went through me and scored. Then Stewart on our side scored twice. Miss Hancock was wearing a bright blue skirt and cheering with Mum and Gerry.

"You were wonderful," Mum said, trying to hug me.

That made it worse. She knows nothing about football. "I wasn't. I was crap."

"Don't use that word, Des."

I pulled away mumbling crap crap crap as I stumbled back to the shed. It was darker in there. I thought there was no-one else there but Mr Burgess, the teacher who just looked at you. His look said change, I thought, and I was about to take my boots off when he knelt down. He never blinked when he looked at you.

"Eye-on-the-ball, Des."

He took me outside and put the ball in front of me. I tried to get it. It vanished.

"I'm not going to be in the net. The ball is. Again."

It disappeared again.

"Again."

It vanished again. When at last I got the ball and managed to tackle him again and again I felt as if I had

had another game of football. I was so tired I couldn't speak.

"Strikers get the glory. But without defenders, they don't win the game. Stopping goals is as important as scoring them." He tapped the ball between his feet. "What do you have to remember?"

"Eye-on-the-ball, Mr Burgess."

He nodded, clapped my shoulder, and was about to take me to mum who was chatting away with Gerry and Miss Hancock when I remembered that other bringing together of words. "Mr Burgess ... What does boo-to-a-goose-mean?"

"Someone's afraid to say something. Or do something." He gave me a funny look, bouncing the ball up-and-down with his hand. "Why do you ask that?"

"Oh ... because of Miss Hancock ..."

"What?" He stopped bouncing the ball. "What about Miss Hancock?"

I told him of how I went to get my hat and I saw Miss Hancock crying.

"Crying? Miss Hancock? Why?"

"She was on the phone to ... to Mr Hunter. She said she didn't want to go out with him ... and mum .... mum said ...

Mr Taylor lost the ball which bounced slowly away from him towards mum, Mr Hunter and Miss Hancock who were laughing together. They stopped when they saw Mr Burgess approaching. I didn't know what he was going to do or say but the three stopped laughing. Mr Burgess's fists were clenched like a boxer's. Miss Hancock picked up the ball. Mr Burgess took it and thanked her. I thought he was going to give Mr Hunter one but he said to him: "I think Des should play full-back Gerry, not mid-field. At mid-field he wants to score. He plays far too far forward."

Going home we saw Miss Hancock and Mr Burgess leaving school together. They were talking so close together they didn't notice us. Mum said I must be so disappointed Mr Burgess didn't want me as a striker. I told her a full-back was as important as a striker and saving a goal was as important as scoring one. I said to her that I told Mr Burgess about hearing Miss Hancock on the phone to Mr Hunter.

"You didn't!"

"Why?"

"I see..."

"See what, mum?" She had told me my bedtime story and I was in that eyes-closing-down-drowsy time.

"Mr Burgess is such a shy man I doubt if he would ever have opened his mouth to her if you hadn't opened your big one."

"What ... what is love ... mum ..."

She may have given me the answer, but I don't know and I still don't know because I fell fast asleep.

Vote for Des

Some school days never end. Friday is bad. Wet Friday when you can't go out to play one of the worst. Worst of all was the one when Miss Hancock rapped on her desk and said: "Politics. What does that mean? Anybody?"

Nobody. Faces staring at desks. Pol-i-tics? Pulled faces. Nobody was interested. Rain on the windows. Stewart pretending his hand was a spider, crawling towards Lucy's dress. The nasty spider began to pull at her dress, showing her knickers. Lucy slapped the spider away but at the same time was giggling.

Miss Hancock rapped on her desk again and turned on the television screen.

"What is this place called?"

Some hands and voices. "Big Ben ... Westminster ..."

Bighead Stewart, of course, got the right answer. "The Houses of Parliament, Miss."

"He wants to be an MP miss," said Lucy.

"Prime Minister," said Stewart.

Lucy giggled again and gave him a look as if he already was. She was his girl friend. Everybody seemed to have a girl friend except me. It seemed to have happened overnight, as everything did in our class. We still watched Horrid Henry but secret messages of what to look at online went round people with the best iPhones.

"Prime Minister?" Miss Hancock said. "Well you can be. Prime Minister of this class at any rate. Today this class is going to be Parliament." She told us some more things about Parliament which sounded the most boring place on earth so I could scarcely keep my eyes open. Until I heard my name.

"What Des did delivering leaflets was politics."

Stewart's hand shot up. "I'll be leader of the Conservatives," he said.

"There are no Conservatives," Miss Hancock said. "Not here. No Labour. There are Orange and Yellow parties."

Politics was about deciding how we wanted to live, Miss Hancock said. What sort of schools we wanted. Did we want *any* schools at all? Everybody was awake now, hands shooting up, voices yelling no no no, nobody wanted no schools no more, let's do without schools!

"Then how would people learn how to do anything? Where would the doctors come from? Who would have got your arm better when you were in hospital, Des?"

Everyone went very quiet. Miss Hancock chalked one word on the board in large letters. POLITICIANS.

"They decide how many teachers, doctors and nurses we want and so on. How would you like to decide something about school on Friday?"

"Go home early," said Stewart.

Everybody laughed until Miss Hancock said: "All right." Silence. "You're deciding. You are Parliament. But you can't lose teaching time. When you're learning something. You'll have to lose break time to make up for it."

I hated the idea of losing break time. I loved them for football. It was soon Des v Stewart. As always. Miss Hancock told us to make speeches. Speeches? I don't know where Stewart got it all from. His voice was big and rang round the classroom.

"Don't you want to be home early?" Stewart said. "Get your homework out of the way? Go away for the weekend? Or watch Netflix? Have more time to yourselves? Or do you want longer break time here? Keep the teachers watching you? What do you want? ...."

Kids were grinning. So was Miss Hancock. Stewart waved his card and said: "Vote for me, your Conservative I mean your Blue - I mean your Yellow Candidate!" and sat down as everyone cheered and thumped their desks. Even I almost started to.

As mum did the meal that evening, I told Almost about Stewart. He was the son of Mike, who owned the garage where Almost worked.

"What happened after Stewart spoke?" Almost said.

"I spoke about how Caleb didn't score for our team."

Mum laughed. "Politics is not about football Des!"

"Mine is!"

She tried to put her arm round me and I pulled away. I hate it when she's like that. "And then?"

"I lost." My cheeks went burning red. I hated losing, particularly to Stewart.

"That's life," Almost said. "It's people like Stewart and his dad who run the country."

"What a stupid thing to say!" mum said.

"It may be stupid but it's true!" he said, "so it's best he gets used to it."

She banged a plate of fish and chips in front of me. "It doesn't have to be true! And I don't think *you* should get used to it either, Almost."

Fish and chips was my fave but I pushed my head forward to listen. More and more Almost was my dad. He was terrific with bikes and footer. But he was not my real dad. I still had, in the bottom of one of my drawers, the story I had written about the papers I had found in my Grandad's house. The police papers about when he had arrested my dad. My real dad. Was he still in prison? I had sworn to finish the story. To find my real dad.

"Where is my dad?" I said.

She was drinking some wine and coughed and spilled some out. " A long way away. I hope."

"Why?"

She didn't answer and turned away,.

"Have you a picture of him?"

She shook her head.

"What's he like?"

She rubbed my hair and laughed, but it was a funny kind of laugh. She said she didn't know him very well, or for very long before they split up then she held me tight and said nothing more.

We ate for a bit and she said: "Politics is not about football Des, its about what we can do for people like Caleb."

"Get him back on form," I said. "He's not been scoring goals as a striker."

"Striker." She turned away and said all quiet to Almost: "More like he's been struck."

"What do you mean, struck?" I said.

"Finish your tea," she said, all sharp.

Caleb was great. He was as crazy about football as I was. But he had had a fall or something and been taken into hospital. He was back now and I expected him to be the same. Fastest runner. Good striker. It was a match where parents came. Caleb used to come with his mum, Maxine. She has a huge laugh. Last time she came with a feller she called Mister Jason. He had cobweb tattoos and a ring in one ear.

"I asked Mister Jason where the other one was."

"You what?" mum said.

"His other ear ring."

"You musn't say things like that!" mum said, but she could hardly get the words out for laughing. "What did he say?"

"He sort of smiled and said ask Caleb."

She stopped laughing. I was in the bath and she soaped me and got all quiet. Almost, who had been laughing at the door got quiet too. He got a screwdriver and tightened the hinge on the door while I dried myself.

"See? It's what I told you about Caleb," she said to him. "What do I do?"

He just kept screwing although the screws looked as tight as could be.

I never wanted to go to bed. I never felt sleepy. I wanted a bit more telly, a game, anything but to go to bed. Once she got me there, though, and started the story, usually I couldn't stop my eyes from closing. But that night was different. She got her story. Opened it. Then instead of reading it she said:

"What did you mean when you said Caleb wasn't on form? He didn't score?"

"Yes. And ..."

"And what Des?"

Her face wasn't her night night face. I never got to the hug stage. She wasn't telling me a story. I was telling her one. How Caleb lost it. It's like learning to read or write, playing football, I told her. For a long time you're so slow and clumsy and think you'll never do it but then you open a book or pick up a pen and you're doing it. The feet find the ball just like that, I told her. Caleb started losing the ball when Mister Jason came. Jason shouted to him to find his left foot and Caleb was right in front of the goal and he couldn't find any foot. My eyes were closing and it was like I was going into a dream as I saw Caleb stumble and almost fall and the ball fly crazily past the goal ...

"He didn't score nothing, " I said. "We'll have to find a new striker."

Mum put her finger to her lips to Almost, who was at the door listening. "See what I mean," she whispered as she went over to him. "Poor Caleb is falling to pieces!"

Falling to pieces? What did she mean? Bits falling off him? I went from one side to another but I couldn't get no sleep. Was it that mum hadn't give me her story? Or that mine was somehow unfinished? I got up, my legs heavy and my lids stuck over my eyes and stumbled towards the kitchen.

"I was working on the ward at the hospital when Caleb was brought in," Mum was saying to Almost. "There were bruises all over his body. A ligament torn. His arm might have been broken."

They were drinking and didn't see me standing at the door.

"What did his mum say?" Almost said.

"Maxine? In hospital? She told the doctor he did it playing football. Football!"

I had never heard her voice so scornful before.

Almost poured some more beer. "Tell your supervisor."

"Mum ..." I started but the telly was on and he was pouring and she was talking with her head in her hands.

"Sister Barker? What can we do about it, she says, if his mother says nothing?"

Almost took a swallow and shrugged "Then what can you do?"

I was about to go into the room when mum said "We can do nothing until Jason kills him? Is that what you mean?"

Was Jason planning to kill Caleb? It was like a story, the sort of story Miss Hancock teaches us to write. But it wasn't no story at all. Not at all. It was like a bad dream. She wasn't like the mum I knew. Just as I'd never heard her voice before, her usual smiling face had gone. She was leaning across the table, grabbing Almost's hand before he took another forkful.

"That's what nearly happened to you didn't it? You were nearly half- killed weren't you? When you were a kid! But in spite of that -"

Almost half-killed? And it was going to happen to Caleb? The room spun round me. I couldn't breathe. I was IN this terrible story. Part of it. I couldn't get out of it. Mum was turning upside down and I was on the floor. Almost was jumping up, knocking over his beer which spilt round me. My legs and arms was going all stiff, one way and another like a puppet doll I once had and Mum was lifting me and she went one way then another and I was on my bed which was floating like a boat and Almost was holding my legs down until my mum's own face came back and her warmth and her safeness and my legs stopped wanting to leave me and the ceiling stayed still.

A doctor at mum's hospital examined me. He said I had a seashore or something and gave me some tablets I must remember to take. In a story for Miss Hancock I wrote I had a seashore. She turned away for a bit and I thought she was laughing although she couldn't have been because it wasn't at all funny.

"I think it might be spelt s-e-i-z-u-r-e, Des."

"Not my seashore," I said. "I was on a boat all at sea."

"Seashore," she said. "Of course! I'm sorry. I see."

The best thing about going back to school was seeing Caleb because I wondered after that bad dream whether I would ever see him again. I wondered if he was dead. It was all a story I had heard! He was getting better at football and he was back in the team to meet our hated rivals High Park school but then he had a fall. He was back in hospital. I was so upset I couldn't get no sleep. I called to mum but Almost was talking so loud she couldn't hear.

"Tell him!" he said.

"Tell Des! Tell him what?"

"What you think is happening to Caleb!"

"Don't be stupid."

"Stupid am I, stupid," Almost said. You keep asking what happened to me. All right I'll tell you. I was almost killed by my drunken father. He was ok when he was sober. He taught me how to repair things. How to use my hands. He could be great. Could be. My mum didn't want anything to happen to him and pretended pretended. Nobody did anything. Nobody said anything. I wouldn't be here if I hadn't killed him."

"*You* killed him?"

I stopped calling out. I couldn't move. I slid down the wall and listened. I couldn't believe what Almost was saying and I couldn't not believe it.

"He was so pissed."

From the hall I could just see them in the kitchen. "He was so pissed that evening. He got on his motor bike. I *knew* he didn't remember we hadn't fixed the brake proper. I started to tell him but I stopped."

He stared out from the kitchen. I thought he had seen me but I don't think he saw anything or anyone just then.

"There was a bad corner from our street on to the main road. I heard the crash. I can still hear it."

He dropped his head into his hands. Mum put her arm round him. His back was shaking. Mum said: "If he was that drunk he wouldn't have taken any notice if you had told him."

"I know. I know. I know ... do you think that makes any difference?"

Did Almost kill his dad? Or was it a story? I no longer knew what was real and what was story. Where I was! Almost joked about everything so much. Next day when he picked me up at school I asked him. He gave me a look, then laughed.

"Who told you that?"

"I heard you last night. In the kitchen. Telling mum."

He had very big hands and the tips of his fingers were always black with oil and dirt. "You're a nosey little sod aren't you. Don't tell your mum I used that naughty word." He laughed again. "I was just having a drink or two last night. Telling mum a story. That's all."

We stopped to cross at a zebra and I was about to go on when a motor bike with *Fast Food* on its big boot roared across. Almost grabbed me by the hand, pulling me back and shouting after the motor cyclist: "You stupid ...!"

He was shaking. Shaking shaking shaking. He kept his hand so tightly round mine it hurt. When I said so he said sorry sorry sorry Des and we went on for a bit without saying anything. Then he stopped. He looked funny. Shifting about from one foot to the other. Chewing a finger nail before speaking.

"Do you want to go and see Caleb?"

"Caleb?" I was looking forward to going home, having the chocolate biscuit that Almost always sneaked to me when Mum wasn't there and watching Horrid Henry.

"He's your friend, isn't he?" He shouted at me as if he was angry about something, I didn't know what. "Well, do you want to see Caleb or not?"

I nodded only because I was frightened and I thought that was what he wanted and he grabbed me by the hand.

When we got to the ward it was suddenly fun. Almost had bought a little motor car for me to give Caleb. The nurse told Almost he would love a visitor. His mum was not due for a bit and I was about to go in and surprise him when Almost stopped me. He was shifting about from one foot to another.

"Ask him ..." he said. "When you're playing with him ... er ... what happened."

"What happened?" We were just by the door and I could see Caleb in bed, bored and restless.

Almost bit his lip so hard a little trickle of blood ran. "When he had his fall..."

Caleb saw me. He shouted my name. I was running towards him when Almost snatched at me, nearly pulling off my T-shirt. "Be a nosey little sod!" he said and went off to the loo, shouting as he did: "Don't tell your mum I used that naughty word!"

"I banged my leg where I banged it afore," Caleb said. Then we tried to put together the car Almost had brought but couldn't. Almost came back and did it. He looked at the plaster on Caleb's leg and asked him what happened.

Caleb had a little snub nose which seemed to grow smaller. He had been laughing away when we were playing but now he spoke in such a small voice you could scarcely hear him. "I fell over," he said.

"What were you doing?" Almost said.

"I was in bed."

"How can you fall over in bed!" Almost sat at the foot of the bed, then dropped on the floor. "The only thing you can break is your bum!"

Caleb and I both laughed and I fell off and held my bum and asked Almost if he could mend it. I was still on the floor when Caleb's mum Maxine came in and pulled me up. When we told her what we were laughing about she clutched her bum and asked Almost if he could mend it. Everybody in the ward laughed because she had such a big one and such a big mop of curly hair.

She and Almost became friends because he was picking me up at school that week and every day he took me to see Caleb. Each day Caleb looked better. His plaster was off and we played footer between the beds until the nurse stopped us.

"I don't wanna go home," he said.

"Why?"

He shook his head. "I don't. I just don't, that's all."

Maxine was there. Getting his clothes ready, talking to Almost. I remembered what he had told me. Be a nosey sod.

"Is it your dad?"

"I haven't got a dad."

"Jackson?"

He nodded. "I was fast asleep ... I had an 'orrible dream. There was bangs. A plosion. I thought the flats was falling down. I jumped out of bed. I wanted mum ..." He stopped and mumbled: "She told me not to say anything. I promised."

A tear trickled down his cheek. Then another.

"You can tell me Caleb. I want you to play for our team."

"I want to. I want - want -" The words would scarcely come out.

"What happened?"

"He kicked me."

"Who?"

Caleb kept swallowing so much he couldn't get the word out.

"Jackson?" I said.

He nodded, tears coming in a rush now, the words gulping out in spurts. "I ... I ... couldn't sleep and I ... I ... I went to mum and and he he ... Jackson was in bed with her ... On top of her ... I don't know what they were doing but he saw me and kicked right out at me kicked me twice like a football and it felt like he'd ... he'd kicked it off and she had to get the ambulance and ... and ..."

I grabbed the tissues for him as we saw Maxine swooping down on him. "Here now Caleb darling ... here's your friend come to cheer you and all those tears!"

I'd never seen Almost so angry when I told him and mum.

"Kicking the poor little kid! I'll sort him out. I'll tell him a thing or two."

"What good will that do?" mum said.

"Jackson'll think twice about touching him again."

"Caleb promised not to tell anyone, " I said.

"So we just wait until he gets hurt again?" Almost said to mum. "That's what you said at the start of all this!"

We went round and round in circles until it was my bedtime. Mum collected my school things for the morning. She pointed to my exercise book. At the top of a page was DEEBATE. The rest of the page was blank.

"It's your turn to speak, isn't it?"

"Is it?"

She gripped the exercise book. I thought she was going to give me one. Then she shoved it into my bag.

"We talked about children on bikes. Safety. Remember?" She got me to write a few more notes and put them in my bag.

In the morning when I woke up I remembered I had to debate. Against Stewart. It was the last thing I wanted to do. "I don't feel very well mum," I groaned.

"D'you want a bacon sandwich or not?" she said.

Almost said he'd have it and that got me up. She dragged clothes on me. It was not only Friday there were dark clouds. Almost had a rotten-looking car from the garage which had been giving him trouble, but it started first time. In the cloakroom she made sure I had my notes and gave me a big hug.

"Good luck, kid."

I really did feel sick but before I could tell her she had gone and Miss Hancock was taking us all down the corridor into the classroom with a clattering of shoes and a banging of desk lids.

"My throat's sore," I said to Miss Hancock.

"Can everyone hear Desmond all right?" Miss Hancock said.

"Yes Miss!" said Stewart. "Loud and clear."

I tripped as I went on the teacher's platform and she caught me. I remembered Mum had made me do my notes ... I would gabble them out and shoot back to my desk.

I felt in my back pocket. All that was in it was a half-chewed mint. I'd left the notes in the cloakroom. Row upon row of children gaped up at me. There seemed twice as many as usual, coughing, shuffling, staring.

Miss Hancock smiled at me. "Desmond Walker, Orange Party. On cycle safety."

I swallowed. I wanted to ask her if could go to the cloakroom for my notes but nothing came out. I seemed to have lost my voice.

Miss Hancock gave me a bigger, even more encouraging smile. "Des."

I couldn't remember a single thing to say. I opened my mouth to ask her if I could go for my notes but right below me was Stewart. He spoke without notes. He folded his arms and smiled up at me. My cheeks were burning. Near Stewart was my desk. Next to it was another empty desk. Caleb's. I pointed to it.

"Caleb .... when is he coming back? When are we going to have him for a striker? When ..."

Miss Hancock smiled, but it was much less of a smile. "We've done football, Desmond. This is about cycle safety ..."

Somebody cheered. Stewart thumped his desk. I don't know where it came from. What happened. It was Stewart's mocking face. And that empty desk of Caleb's.

"Yes ... er Miss ... Yes er ... We did ... used to go to school on bikes with Max, Maxine, Caleb's mum ..."

I just remembered. How boring she was! She used to stop us in the flat-yard before we went out on the cycleway. I just said it as she said it.

"Helmet ... is it tight? ... strap not twisted ... half of all the injuries are all to face and forehead ... lights ... Do they work? ... Do you have your key to your bike lock, Des?"

There it was! Still swinging by a chain to my belt. I swung it as I used to, almost hitting Miss Hancock. Everybody giggled. I went through the performance Maxine made us go through every time before she took us to school. I would still be grumpy and half-asleep, waggling the key, checking that the lights worked. Then, while we were on the cycle-way, she wouldn't let us go side by side talking football if she thought it was too narrow.

I wobbled about as if I was on a bike, shouting warnings as Max used to: "Car door! ... car door! ... "

The class clapped. Miss Hancock did. Even Stewart clapped. Somebody cheered. I was dizzy with it. Happy with it.

"Well done, Des!" Miss Hancock said as I was about to leave the platform. "Yet Caleb had a cycle accident, didn't he?"

"No. He was hit."

It just came out. There had been so much talk, argument about between Almost and Mum about what had happened the words just came out.

"Hit ... What do you mean, Des?"

She was the teacher. I had to answer her. "By Mr Jason."

She stared at me. The whole class stared at me. At Caleb's empty desk. Then she said you mean he didn't have any accident on the cycle track?

"No Miss," I muttered.

She told me to sit down and I thought it was all for-gotten. I felt like Desmond Taylor MP as she chalked up all the points I had made. There were a lot of arguments about sometimes you had to go on pavements and I won as the Orange cos I remembered one time Maxine counting ten cars parked on cycle tracks. What else could you go on but the pavement?

I ran from the classroom shouting "Order Order ..." towards Almost, who was picking me up.

"Desmond!" Miss Hancock called me back, with Almost.

"Have you parked on a cycle way?" I said to him.

"Nowhere else to park," he muttered. "Is she going to tell me off?"

It wasn't that.

"I know," she said, Desmond is very good at telling stories ..."

"What has he done now?" Almost said.

Miss Hancock twisted her hands together. She swallowed. "And ... and that Caleb is in bed with a bad fracture ... Desmond told me ... well ... he told me and the whole class that he was hit by his mother's boy friend ..."

"He was." Almost said.

He went off like he did before with Mum. Like grown-ups always do they seemed to forget I was there. It sounded more horrible than I already knew. He said that Mr Jason had hit her as well. I remembered the bad bruise on her face which she said happened when she fell off her bike.

"Why doesn't she leave him?" Miss Hancock said.

"Leave him?" Almost said. "It's his flat! She's nowhere else to go!"

"Caleb stayed with me one night," I said.

They suddenly seemed to remember I was there. Almost coughed and blew his nose. Miss Hancock straightened a chair and put some exercise books in her briefcase.

"Yes ... yes ..." Almost said. "Caleb stayed ... they played football on the telly and wouldn't let us watch it ..."

"Desmond did very well in Parliament," Miss Hancock said. "Won his vote on cycle safety."

"Pity it never does anything for people like Maxine and Caleb," Almost burst out.

When we got to his car a parking ticket was fluttering under the windscreen wipers. He ripped it off, crumpled it up and flung it in the back of the car. "Fat lot of good that did!" he said.

It was about six weeks later, the very worst day of the year - going back to school after the long summer holiday. I didn't want to get up. Didn't want to go to school. There was bright sun through the window. The sun wasn't going back to school. Why should I?

"Up!" Almost cried, pulling me out of my bed. "We have to work - why shouldn't you?"

He pulled my bike out of a cupboard. I hadn't been using it because of a puncture. He mended it.

"I thought you were supposed to be the expert on cycle safety ... it hasn't been oiled ... this brake is soft ..."

They were on at me because I'd only just started breakfast and Mum wanted to go early. Bump bump bump, rattle rattle rattle as I took my clanky old bike down the steps. Mum went on a cycle-way I didn't know.

"This isn't the way to school mum!" I said.

"It's the way I go," she said.

Grown-ups. They always think they know best. The sun came out from behind clouds, bright and warm. She was going down another street I didn't know. There was a big rambling house with a notice *Womens' Aid*. In a large yard bikes were parked.

Mum thumped at the door. It was opened by Maxine with the biggest smile I had ever seen. She hugged mum. A football hit me with a force that knocked me over. It had been kicked by Caleb.

I yelled at him: "Can you play?"

"Been practicing my left foot mate!"

Maxine told us no men were allowed. They had their own room and could cook there.

"Thanks to you and Almost," she said. There were tears shining in her eyes.

If she was happy I didn't know why she was crying but I didn't care. All I cared about was we had our striker back. And at the end of our first day we were desperate to get to the park to practice our first game against Stewart's team but Maxine kept waiting to talk to Miss Hancock to thank her for her new bedsit.

"Me?" Miss Hancock said. "You must thank Parliament."

"Parliament?" said Maxine, with a puzzled frown.

"He did it." Miss Hancock pointed to me. "The Leader of the Orange Party." Miss Hancock pointed to me.

I did it? Sometimes I think I'll never understand school. Ever. But I never mind it when teacher gives me a good mark.

Looks and No-Looks

She was stupid, Em. Like most girls. First of all her best friend was Lucy, Stewart's girl. That was bad enough. Then she didn't like footer. She dressed all weird in ripped skinny leggings or funny skirts in layers. And then she stuck her nose in the air and had a posh-voiced mum with a big Jeep.

That day, when Almost picked me up from school, her mum Mandy was trying to start the car. Almost went to help her, opened the bonnet and shook his head. He said it needed an ignition and spark or something. While he was closing the bonnet she phoned a taxi, groaned and said she couldn't wait that long.

"Where you've to get to?" said Almost.

"Lyceum," she said.

He told them to jump in his car then, during the journey, she had a phone conversation in which she said couldn't stay. She had to take her child home.

"Em could come home with us if you like." Almost said.

"Oh! ... Really? ... I'll only be half-an-hour seeing someone. Do you mind Em?"

I saw in the mirror Em hated the idea as much as I did but Mandy was one of those people who never wait for an answer.

'Thank you ever so much! That's *so* kind of you Almost!" She gave him the sort of smile that seems to make men do what she wants. When Em was in our flat I didn't know what to say to her. I couldn't even look at her. Mum was doing evening shift at the hospital and it was Almost who offered her a biscuit.

"No thank you".

"Tea?"

She shook her head, looked in the fridge, saw a raspberry sorbet which was mine. Before I could stop her she had the top off. And I don't know how she got it, with our manky old telly, but she clicked on Masterclass programme about teenage singers and sat there watching it, licking my sorbet, when I wanted to watch football.

"What do you want to do all that for?" I whispered to Almost in the kitchen.

"Customer," he said. "Jeep. Expensive to repair." Like he was always doing, he twiddled his finger and thumb together and winked. "Money, kid. You'll learn"

"Why bring Em here?"

"She's your friend!" Almost said.

"No. She's not! I don't even know her!"

"Rubbish. She's in your class!"

I took one more look at her sitting in my chair, watching my telly, scraping out the last of my sorbet and grabbed the programme planner. I was about to turn the telly off when Almost snatched the planner back, slapped his hand over my mouth, and made a threatening gesture - all behind Em's back. She half turned but I plunged away and slammed into my bedroom.

Almost was rotten. I thought he was like a new dad but he wasn't! He was horrible horrible *horrible!* I buried my head in the pillow, I thought he would come in and see me at least but he never. I could hear him talking, laughing - *laughing* with that cow of a girl!

"Done some spag bol, Des. Wash your hands."

The telly went off. It was all quiet in there. I went to the door and heard the clink of plates and knives and forks. They must be in the kitchen. The smell of the food came to me. Spag Bol was one of my favourites. I could hear him approaching. He was going to come in my room. I would eat it there. That would show them!

"Des!" he shouted from some distance.

I ignored him.

"Do you want some or not?"

"N-oooooooooooooo!" I yelled.

"Suit yourself." I heard her say something and him answer: "Napkins are in that drawer there."

Napkins. Napkins! *Naper-kins!* When Almost first came to live with us that slob with his dirty greasy fingers scarcely used a knife and fork, let alone napkins. I flung myself back on the bed and buried my head under the pillow again to try and stop hearing them but they were laughing together too loud and the sound of food being scraped from the pan made my tummy rumble horribly. I couldn't bear it. I went to the door but before I opened it the bell rang. At last! Em would go! I would get the last of the Spag Bol. Ignore Almost. But they talked and laughed and talked and then Almost shouted.

"Des! Come and see what Mandy has brought you!"

Mandy! Almost even made his voice sound different. I heard him coming towards the door and ran back towards my bed, banging my foot against it, biting my lip to stop me howling from pain before crashing down.

"I know you're not asleep. Look." He was holding a pair of jeans.

I was opening my mouth to yell at him to go away when I saw Mandy right behind him.

"I'm terribly sorry if we woke you up," she began then stopped, giving me a funny look. "I thought he was," she said to Almost. "You're just over four feet aren't you?"

"Am I?" I said.

"An inch. Perhaps an inch and a half even. Stand up."

Somehow, in spite of what I felt, her tone of voice made you do what she wanted. "Put these on," she said, taking the jeans from Almost and holding them out to me.

"Jeans?" I said. I felt like I should be putting on pyjamas.

"Skin-Legs," said a voice at the door. It was Em, leaning against the jamb, arms folded. As she spoke she rolled her eyes at me and looked at the ceiling.

I took off my old, crappy jeans, which got tighter and more torn every day I wore them and pulled on Skin-Legs. They seemed made for me. Mandy told me to turn round and asked her daughter what she thought. Em stared at me in a way that made my cheeks burn. She nodded.

"Mind if I take a photograph?" Mandy said.

As usual, she never waited for an answer. From a big bag round her shoulder she took a camera.

"Smile, please." she said.

I scowled.

"Do you have a smile?" she said.

I was getting fed up with her and stuck out my tongue. Em bit her cheeks, just managing to stop herself from laughing. There was a brilliant flash. I was so startled I almost fell. Em burst out laughing. Encouraged, I did the jump, skip jumps we were doing before football.

Flash! Flash! Flash!

They kept on shouting for me next morning for breakfast. I couldn't get up. When I did I could hardly open my eyes. Neither could mum after working all night at the hospital. Almost did all the talking.

"Wears smashing clothes."

"Who?" Mum grunted.

"Mandy. Em's mum."

"Oh. Her." She blinked as Almost pushed the print of a photograph across the table. "Who's that?"

"Your son."

Now her eyes opened wide. "What on earth is he wearing?"

"Skin-Legs."

She pushed it away. "Did he do his arithmetic homework?"

"Er ... " Almost looked at me.

"Des?"

I sloshed more milk in my plate and lifted it to my mouth. I was starving. He'd done me a bit of a meal when Em and her mum left but there was hardly any spag left.

Mum brought my plate back to the table, spilling half of it. Almost got a cloth.

"*Did* you?" Mum said to me.

"I'll do it tonight. I promise."

"You promised last night!" she said, as if she was speaking to both of us. "I honestly don't know what to do with you. Both of you!"

"Mandy is a photographer. Fashion," Almost said.

"I know what my lady does," she said.

"Why do you call her my lady?" I said.

"Don't you dare call her that!" she said.

Her eyes were closing again. She gripped the arms of her chair. If Almost could take me to school, she said, she would go straight to bed.

"I promised to phone Mandy about Des's photo-shoot," Almost said.

"His *what*?" That woke her up all right.

"Photo-shoot. For Skin Legs."

"Photo-shoot?"

"They're looking for a eight-year old to model some boys' clothes."

"When?"

"Friday."

"That's a school day!"

"I said -"

"You can unsay it. He's my son, not yours. He's not doing it and that's flat."

"Jess - "

"Get your coat on!" she said to me. "You'll be late for school as it is. I'll take him."

Miss Hancock gave me a black mark because I didn't hand in my maths. She said I would have to miss break-time to do them and left me in the empty class-room. I didn't care. Maths was *stupid*. Em came back long before break ended. I had not answered a single question. I didn't care. I told Em about the blow-up between Mum and Almost.

"Can't you do the photo-shoot for my mum?" Em said.

I shook my head. I didn't care about that either. I wanted to go back home to mum. I could still see her standing in the yard while Almost grabbed me and shoved me in the car. I wondered if she was still there. I wanted to go home. I never ever wanted to go to that stupid *stupid* school again.

"My mum will be so disappointed," she said.

Who cared about her mum or Em or 6 x 4 = 34. The computer did it all for us these days.

"Please," she said. Will you do the photo-shoot for my mum, please? Des?"

She called me Des. My name. Me. Des. I liked that.

"I can't. I can't do these maths. I'll have to stay in - "

"Twenty-four." she said.

"What?"

"Six times four is twenty-four."

I could do some of the pluses. Then there were the circle two numbers togethers to add up to ten. After she showed me how, I managed to do them. By the time we heard them coming in from the playground and Miss Hancock was in the corridor, Em slipped away.

There had been some argument in the playground - but for once I hadn't been there and couldn't have been part of it. Miss Hancock came in with her fed-up face and it grew longer as she approached my desk. She stared at my answers.

"Well, well Desmond Taylor," she said. It just shows what you can do when you try."

As well as drawings, Em could do voice imitations. Waiting to be collected after school she deepened her voice and said: "Well, well, Desmond Foster, it just shows what you can do when you try."

Just then, I felt I could do anything. "I can do stories, maths, photo-shoots..."

"I hope," Em said.

"Nothing to it! You just stand there."

She made a face. "I can't do it. There's a rotten woman -"

She told me. It was the bright light. You stood there doing nothing for hours then you had to do everything in five minutes.

"The photoshoot on Friday is with this woman," she said. "There's more and more work coming for kids and - "

She stopped as she saw my Mum coming towards us. I had expected it to be Almost and I wondered what had happened. Em nudged me. "Ask her," she whispered.

"Mum," I began. "There's this photo -"

"Come on. Desmond! I'm working again tonight.."

"Can you just speak to Em about -"

"Please! Sorry Em. Sorry. I can't stop."

She grabbed me by the hand, walking swiftly towards the gates. I didn't know what to say. What to do. She was practically pulling me off the street. Through the railings I could see Em staring after us. On the other side of the street was Em's mum chatting to somone. She began to smile and wave towards us. I managed a wave but Mum pretended not to see her and dragged me along.

What had I done? Something had happened. It was always me. Always Desmond. I was never Des when they were like this. Almost said nothing. Mum said nothing. Only the telly and next door's telly said anything. I watched Horrid Henry. Mum switched it off half-way through the story. I snatched up the programmer. I saw the look on her face and flung it across the room.

She put her outdoor coat on to go night duty. "His meal's on the table," she said to Almost.

"I have to phone Mandy," Almost said. "Em's mum. To tell her if he can do the photo-shoot."

"No. I told him he couldn't do it until he did his homework."

I jumped up. *"I have done it!"*

She shook her head and opened the door to go. "I want no more stories," Desmond Taylor. No more lies."

"I have! Look!" I pulled out the marked homework with Miss Hancock's ticks and "Very good, Des."

"Well done!" Almost said. "My goodness, I couldn't do all that!"

I saw the look on mum's face. I know mum and she knows me. "What's five times four?" she said,

"Er ... thirty."

Her look did not change. "I mean forty."

"Oh Des," she said. It was cos she called me Des and looked so sad and tired I burst into tears and she put her arms round me and I told her Em had helped me so I could do the photo-shoot. She wiped my eyes and kissed the top of my head.

"Give it a touch of microwave before he eats it," she said to Almost, and went.

Almost caught the door and followed her down the stairs. "After what has happened," he said. "This would be a real help if he did it. D'you realise how much he'd get paid ... well we'd get ... d'you realise?"

"Give him his meal before it's ruined," she said and hurried downstairs.

After what has happened? What was he talking about? Had I heard right? Had there been some kind of bust-up between Almost and mum? He usually let me watch some telly before going to bed but now he wouldn't let me. He shoved me off to bed and I started calling him Never to myself - he would *Never* be my dad when I couldn't get no sleep. I tossed and turned and got up, wanting mum, forgetting she was not there. He was on the phone and shouted at me to get back to bed. When he woke me up in the morning I felt I'd had no sleep at all.

I was glad that mum, although she'd been working all night, said she was taking me to school. It was like we were both sleep-walking. Mum took me into the class where Em was sitting at the front. She said something to Miss Hancock.

Miss Hancock took off her glasses and stared down at me.

"Friday? For a photo-shoot? Well, Mandy has taught here so he'd have a teacher with him. Mmm, Friday is arithmetic day ... but he got such a good mark this week ..."

Looks.

I could feel Em looking at me. I couldn't look at her for I was looking at mum and mum was looking at me. I shut my eyes for I knew what mum was going to say.

"So it is all right if he goes on Friday for the photo-shoot?"

"Check with the head, but it is perfectly all right with me, Mrs Taylor."

I looked at mum but as she hurried out of the class-room she didn't look at me.

Looks. And No-Looks.

Wild Boy

It was cold. Dark. The duvet had fallen off. I tried to drag it back on. It was pulled away by mum who yanked me off the bed as I struggled to get back.

"Up!"

I could still see the moon. "It's night!"

"You wanted work," she said, pulling my jamas off and dragging a T-shirt on. "This is it. Welcome to work."

I stumbled as I tried to get both legs into one hole of my jeans. "Poor Des." She pulled me to her. She was so warm and comfortable and smelt so much of mum my eyes closed tight and I was nearly asleep again.

"You can't go back to sleep! Mandy is here!"

Mandy strapped me in the car and started to drive off. Mum called her back. She beckoned to her to get out of the car. They were talking to each other as grownups do when they don't want you to hear. That woke me up all right. I slid out of my seat belt and pushed the window down.

" ... I've got to pick up Em from school ..." Mandy was saying.

"I don't want Des near the school today," Mum said.

"I'll pick Des up!" Almost was shouting, leaning out of the flat window.

Mum saw me leaning out of the car window and hurried over fumbling to put my seat belt back on.

I wanted to see Em. "Why don't you want me near school?"

"Because," she said. She was red in the face and she kept trying to put my seat belt in the wrong slot. "Because it would be too much for one day." Her eyes were blotchy and I think she had been crying.

"It's that one," I said, pointing to the right slot. She clicked it in. "Be a good Catwalk Des." She hugged me then turned away.

It had been an old theatre. There was a stage with lights so bright you had to turn your head away. There was banging and clattering and people shouting at one another and ignoring you and pushing past you and putting big pictures up. Mandy took me to this woman she called Zoe who had very long legs and a very short skirt that almost wasn't a skirt and who gave me a smile that wasn't a smile.

"Lift your head Wes," she said.

"Des," said Mandy.

Zoe gripped my chin and lifted my head. Her nails were bright red and sharp. She turned me one way, then another as if I wasn't a person then shouted to the men putting up pictures of people drinking and laughing at white tables. I was pulled into a room with a child's scooter, a football and heaps of other toys. I went to play with them but before I could a girl came in, said I must be Wes and put me in a T-shirt with jagged lettering WILD BOY.

She pulled me into jeans so tight they split at the ankles. She stared at me then tore them even more.

I said I was thirsty and she said coke? then Zoe called her and I never saw her again. It was suddenly quiet. The T-shirt was thin but the room was so hot drop after drop of sweat trickled down me.

I came out into the studio. People were huddled in small groups. Then I saw Mandy knelt with her cameras on her. Above her Zoe was pointing, walking, telling people what to do.

Someone touched my shoulder. It was another WILD BOY, some years older than me.

"What happens now?" I said.

"Nothing," he said. He took a sip from a paper cup. He had an iPhone with cords running up to his ears. He tapped at it and jigged from one foot to another.

"Nothing?"

He jigged and shrugged. "Most of the time. Who cares? We get paid for it."

"Do we?"

He took out the ear-phones and looked at me for the first time. He had very narrow black eyes and dark curly hair. "You new?"

"Yes."

He stared more closely at me. There was something funny about his look. "I wonder ..." He looked towards Zoe, who was suddenly shouting at everybody.

"Wonder what?" I said.

He shook his head and took a swallow from his cup. I asked him where I could get a drink. He suddenly smiled. He had a much nicer smile than I was expecting. He told me he'd get me one and went to a machine I could now see in the shadows by the stage. I drank the coke in one gulp and got another. He told me his name was Jake. As well as Mandy there were television cameras. I stared at them sliding silently over the floor. I shut my eyes and opened them to make sure I wasn't in a dream. This was better than school. Much much better! If I did this I would never have to add up or answer questions for Miss Hancock again!

There was a lot of noise again as what Jake called the set was finished. The scene was a room in a cafe where a Mum and Dad had a meal with Wild Boy who was driving them crazy.

"I can do that all right," I said.

Jake bounced a football. A woman who looked a bit like a teacher, wearing a striped blouse and skirt, came up to him and wished him good luck.

"I'd leave the ball alone if I were you, Jake."

"It's not mine Steph," he said, looking all innocent-like and bouncing it towards me. As she turned away, he stuck his tongue at her back and winked at me. I caught the ball as Zoe shouted at us. Jake put his finger to his lips.

"Don't do it yet."

"What?"

"Take the ball from me, then dribble it round their table. Don't let anyone take it from you. Then all you have to do is *not* do as you're told. Get it?"

"Oh, yeh. I can do that all right. Great."

He pointed to a table where there was a large birthday cake with a number of burning candles. A girl with a bright smile which never left it stood, preparing to cut it.

"Action!" Zoe shouted.

Jake dropped the ball. "Go for it! At the table! Run!"

I went for it. It was terrific. Like football. People were shouting at me. I nearly went into a television camera, veered round, almost fell then Mandy was in front of me yelling at me to stop stop stop. I moved as if I was going left but when Mandy tried to grab me I went right, colliding into the table. The woman with a knife lurched forward, a piece of cake she had cut coming towards me. I grabbed the piece of cake, knocking Zoe down. Someone grabbed the ball.

"You little idiot!" Mandy shouted. "Why did you do that?"

She was so angry I just stood there clutching the piece of cake, not knowing what I had done wrong. Hadn't I been wild enough? Done enough wrong? Spoilt enough cake?

"Jake told me to - " I began.

Mandy clapped her hands to her face. "Oh! I see it all now! You should never listen to him."

Jake was curled up, helpless with laughter. He kept trying to stop, then collapsing into laughter again. Mandy went to help pick up Zoe. Coffee was spilt over her skirt. "Oh Zoe ... I'm so, so sorry ... I don't know what to say ..."

Zoe went to the cameraman. "Did you cut?"

The cameraman flung up his hands in despair. "No ... I didn't know what to do ... I just let it run ... !"

Mandy was pulling me away when Zoe said sharply: "Leave Wes."

"Des," said Mandy.

Zoe bent over towards me. Her hand came up and I flinched as I was sure she was going to bash me one but she took some of the cream from the cake and smeared it round my mouth.

"Shoot him," she said to Mandy and the cameraman. "Shoot Wes. As he is."

I did the same run as I had done before, but not half so good. I couldn't do it so badly when I was told to do it as when I wasn't, if you see what I mean.

"Cut!" Zoe yelled.

It was a word I was going to hear a lot of that day. Zoe was worse than any teacher, much much worse. She told me to go back to the mark again and again until I did lose it and hated her and ran to get out of the place, colliding with a screen.

"Keep that," Zoe said. "That's ok. You hate me, don't you?"

I just stared at her, wanting to belt her one. I would have done if I'd had any breath left.

"That's it Wes! That's it! Remember that face!"

I fell on to a bench. It was hot and bright. Sweat was pouring down me. I tried to get up out of the bright lights but an operator squeezed my shoulder and held me where I was. I told him I wanted to go but he told me "Not just yet sonny" giving me a big smile and pushing a Coke into my hand. Everyone was giving me big smiles except Jake who was in a shadowy, cool-looking corner with Stephanie and another woman.

I went towards them. "When are you going to do it, Jake?"

He stared at me, pushing past Stephanie so that she stumbled and almost fell.

"Me? Me?" His hair was wild, his face twisted. Flecks of spit hit my face as he shouted at me. "Are you joking?"

I just stood there, bewildered. "Why? What have I done?"

"What have you done? You bastard ... you've taken my fucking job!"

He came towards me. My Coke flew up in the air as his fist just missed my face and hit my shoulder and I don't know what would have happened if the operator and another hadn't come between us. The room spun round me. Jake was being led out of the room.

"Costume and make-up. Change him. Don't lose that! I can use that!" Zoe shouted.

I couldn't say anything for a bit. There always seemed to be somebody else dressing me, putting make-up on me. Make-up! I said I could dress myself, thank-you, and only women put make-up on. There was a big bruise on my shoulder and a nurse checked me. I said I wanted to go home but nobody took any notice. Women sometimes kissed me and men patted me on the shoulder as if I was a dog.

After a while I was too tired to say anything and did as I was told for what felt like forever until Zoe called: "Ok. That's a wrap!"

Suddenly no-one took any notice of me at all. They didn't look at me. They just seemed to forget completely about me. Mandy said Almost was picking me up very shortly but she had to pick up Em.

It was after five o'clock, well after school leaving and I'd been up since six. Was it Almost or Mum or anyone who was going to collect me? The clattering from the floor began to die down and my eyes began to close.

Did I hear the footsteps in the corridor. I certainly smelt the cigarette. It was Stephanie. She stared at me, as she put out a cigarette.

"Wes."

I'd given up telling them over what felt like a year ago what my real name was.

"Who's with you, Wes?"

"Me."

"Where's your chaperone?"

My eyes half-opened. "Chap ... er ... one?"

She closed her eyes for a moment. She looked as tired as I felt. She sat opposite me and said nothing while two people clattered down the corridor saying goodnight. She looked somehow different. Or was she looking at me somehow different?

"Have you an agent?"

"Agent?"

She took a pad from her shoulder bag and a pen from its clip. "How old are you?"

"Ten."

Her face didn't change a muscle. "How old are you, Wes?"

"Nine and a quarter. And one week."

"Have you done this before?"

"This?"

She waved her hand towards the set. "Modelling? Acting?"

I shook my head, sinking further down in my seat. After that day I never ever wanted to do it again. "I want to be a footballer."

There was the clang and rattle of an opening door and the clatter of boots I recognized.

"Des!" Almost yelled.

My real name! That woke me up all right. Almost was in his end-of-day filth. I ran to him and jumped into his arms, surprising him, surprising myself, but I didn't know what was happening I'd stopped believing that anyone was going to collect me, if I was ever going to go home. Even my name had changed. I snuggled up to him, to the smell of the oil and grease on his overalls. He didn't know how to hold me like Mum did and I had to grab his straps when I slipped and almost fell.

"Hey hey hey hey hey ..." he mumbled. He was put out by all this snuggling. "He's done in aren't you ... what have you been doing to him?"

Stephanie came over to us. "I was beginning to wonder what you are doing to him. Are you his Dad?"

"No no no," I mumbled. "He's Almost."

"We thought he was with Mandy," Almost said. "I've just called on her."

She spelt his name out as she wrote it on her pad. "A- l-m-o-s-t."

Almost didn't like that. I could tell he had had what he called one of those days at the garage. He shifted from one boot to another.

"Poor kid's nackered. Give me his money and I'll take him home."

Stephanie coughed. Another note on her pad. "It isn't quite as easy as all that."

Almost didn't like that. He took a couple of steps towards her. "What isn't quite as easy as all what?"

"Well ..." She ticked off points as she made them. "For a start, he didn't do what he was commissioned to do, but rather more ... " Tick. "Secondly ..." Tick. "I don't know if you realise it, but you're breaking the law by - "

Any mention of breaking the law was enough to get Almost going. "You are breaking the law by not paying us!" he said. "I'm taking this child home."

Miss 10%

Home. Home. The sight of the old car was home. The smell of it as he opened the door crashed me out to sleep before the belt was fastened. Home. The flats. The lift that didn't work. Almost carrying me up the flights of stairs. Was the argument a dream? His mum's voice carrying that end of the day weariness, each word dropping singly out of her mouth.

"I told you how ... to deal with ... people like that."

"It's how she dealt with me!" Almost said.

There was something about money. Or no money. And something about arithmetic. There was something about had I done the last of the arithmetic, since I was just a stand in and a lot of it was just waiting - what Mandy called "hanging around." I hadn't done it. Worse. I had left my school books on the set.

By now it was the next day. Nearly afternoon when I woke up. I discovered it was Saturday. I had missed my football! Everybody was arguing with everyone else. I wanted to go to the park for the last of the football and Mum said I had to go back to the stinking set for my homework when the bell rang.

It was Mandy and Em. I wanted to speak to Em but Mum said no. I had to go to the set and find that work. I tried to get to the speaker but Almost grabbed me and when I had a go at him twisted my arms behind my back. I cried and went into my room and couldn't stop crying.

She came back almost immediately, snatching up things from the floor. "You can stop that. Tidy your room."

Tidy my room? I stopped crying and stared. Mum was hurtling round the kitchen, putting dishes away. Almost was picking up his boots from the living room floor. He never, ever, picked up his boots.

"Shut those drawers!" she snapped at me. "Madam is coming up."

Mandy and Em had never been here. They lived in Forest Park. The posh bit with big gardens.

"So what," Almost muttered. "I don't give a monkey's." Yet he put away his boots, shoved the chair over the hole in the tattered carpet as they rapped at the door because the bell, like most other things, didn't work. I found myself shutting drawers, although I had to open them again because clothing was caught and one drawer was broken and hung out and made it look worse than before.

I went in, half-dressed, still half-asleep. Mandy was staring at me as if I was still on the set.

"Terrific," she said.

Em was giving me a big smile. She flung one fist in the air. In our signals this meant: Keep going! You've got this! Is that what she was saying? I had no idea what I'd got. What was going on.

"I gather you've had a bit of a discussion with our dear Stephanie?" Mandy said to Almost.

"She wouldn't give us the money," he muttered.

"Good for you!" she said. "Screw as much out of them as you can. While you can. They were all trying to get rid of him."

"Who was trying to get rid of who?" Mum said.

"His agent Stephanie, Zoe the director, all of them had had it up to here with Jake ... Look ...." She produced a folder. Another Wild Boy stared out at me, older, with a cake-cream moustache, hair as spiky as the T-shirt lettering and split jeans.

"Who's that?" I said.

"You!" Em cried. "You, *you* big idiot! Wes!"

"Me?"

There were pictures of Wes dancing, swinging from a trapeze, falling from a bike.

I was gradually beginning to wake up. "That's not me."

"Of course it's you, Des." Mandy said. "And I mean it's not you ... it's Wes. You're an actor."

"A what ...?"

Em pulled me into a corner. "You've got a job. You can do things." She whispered into my ear. "Find your dad."

"Find my - "

"Ssshhh!"

Almost shifted in his chair. "What about the money?"

Mandy stared at the photographs. Her lips pursed. "I reckon Jake was getting four hundred."

"Four hundred what?"

"Pounds."

"For what?"

"For the day's shoot."

Mum stared at her for a moment before getting up from her chair. There was a crack from the seating which slipped out of joint. Automatically, as she always did, she put it back into place. "Can I ... can I get anyone a cup of tea? And biscuits?"

Mum wouldn't let me play football in the park after school. I had to go into town. She yelled at me for getting my clothes messed up.

"He's all right," Almost said. "He's Wild Boy."

I didn't think he was Almost at first. He wasn't in his usual overalls. He was wearing a pair of jeans and a jacket I hadn't seen before. Neither had I seen a bright lipstick Mum kept checking on the tube. We got out at Covent Garden. I thought it was a veggie market but there were streets of posh-looking offices. People rushing to go home knocked into us before we found *Steph's Talent*.

The lift worked. There were carpets. Thick carpets. We had to wait. I was almost asleep again by the time she showed us into her office. The walls were covered with pictures of childrens shows: Disney, Harry Potter, Mary Poppins. Stephanie never stopped talking. She said to Almost she was so sorry they had a little bit of a difference, but a child actor had to be licenced, and have a minimum of three hours of school a day ...

Mum poked me sharply in the ribs, catching me as I almost fell off the chair.

"For that shoot he will get three hundred," Stephanie said. "Less ten percent. My commission."

"Ten percent!" Almost said, his jaw dropping. He was about to go on when mum dug him in the ribs.

Stephanie put down the pen which she always had in her hand. There was a rap at the door. A man looked in, raised his hand and went. It was very quiet now. I was fully awake now for what felt like the first time in a week. I realised that Mum and Almost were holding copies of a file. Stephanie tapped what looked to be the same file on her desk.

"Ten percent for getting him work," she said.

"Fine," Mum said. "Fine." She signed.

"I have to ask this," Stephanie said. "Are you married?"

"No," Almost said.

"Are you a civil partnership?" Mum shook her head. "You co-habit?" She nodded.

The pen was back in Stephanie's hand. Almost was staring at the carpet.

"I should inform Wes's father," Stephanie said. "Could you give me his address?"

I leaned forward. I was more than fully awake now.

"I don't have his address." Mum said. "I have no idea where he is." She put the contract back on the desk.

Stephanie made a note, then pushed the contract over to me. "And can you sign it here, Wes, please ..." Stephanie said.

"Des," I said. "Des." As she pointed to where I should sign I remembered what Em had said. This boring looking piece of paper with long difficult sentences was a job. Work. I had a job. Was someone. Could do things. We were high up and through the window I saw the lights of Piccadilly Circus going down Regent's Street towards the river. Somewhere in London was my Dad. I could find him. I didn't have a pen and I borrowed hers and signed, very slowly and carefully, where her finger was pointing.

"He's in prison," I said. "I don't know where, but he's somewhere in prison."

The Wizard of the Forest

I knew it was me but somehow it wasn't me. That summer, a number of times I did Wild Boy filming. There was a picture of me in the paper jumping in the air and a journalist asked me if I had run away from home and "everything" and he seemed disappointed when I said no, I would never run away from my mum. He wrote things I couldn't remember saying, about longing to be an actor and a dancer, and he said I was a True Wild Boy. In fact, far from being wild, at school I was so tired Miss Hancock started calling me Quiet Boy. At home, instead of wanting to play out, I fell asleep in front of the telly. If this was work, I wanted to stay at school.

It wasn't until filming was over I became wilder. The Wild Boy had somehow become me. Or I had become him. It was almost dark at school collection time. Mum collected me with Em and we walked through the park on the way home. Mum stopped to talk to a friend. It was just before Halloween and we could see the huge dark shape of the fire that had been built for bonfire night. I made a broomstick from a few twigs and some cord. They had a much fancier broomstick on the film set where I flew to the moon and back.

"There's a witch over there," I said.

"There's no such things as witches," Em said.

"I'll show you. Follow me."

I started to walk towards the clump of trees near the dark shape of the unlit fire. A bird suddenly fluttered. Em screamed and grabbed my arm.

"We're not to go further away. The gates are closing."

She was nervous, like all girls. "Come on Em! Look. There's the broomstick!"

It grew a lot darker towards the clump of trees. Mum called me. I felt a sudden urge to hide. I was fed up of doing what I was told. Since I was Wild Boy I did much more of what I was told to do than I ever did before. "I'm not coming looking for you!" Mum shouted.

"We're here!" Em yelled and ran towards Mum.

Stupid girl! I would creep round a different way and scare the shit out of them. There was a thicker clump my clothes caught in. I had to tear it free. It was even darker when I came out and I couldn't see a path.

There was the snap of a twig behind me. I whirled round. "Hello?"

Something moved. I heard a rustle and saw a glint of light among a bank of leaves at the foot of a big tree. I stopped, shivering. There was a scuttle and then a squirrel ran up a tree. I told myself not to be as stupid as Em.

"Des?" Mum called. She was getting closer. I'd show her! My eyes were getting better in the dark. I could see the bushes and was beginning to hide under them when I saw a shape. The flutter, the curve of her wings. It looked exactly like a witch in one of the films I had done.

"Wild Boy?"

It was a man's voice. He came out of the shadow of a tree. He had a jacket slung over his shoulders which

I had taken for wings. As he came towards me I scrambled out from under the bushes, starting to run but he stopped and I turned. How did he know I was Wild Boy? I wasn't wearing the shirt. He had a hat pulled over a very pale face. Mum called again.

"You'd better go," he said. "Des. Or is it Wes?"

"Des?" mum called again.

"Call her," the man said. "Tell her you're coming."

I shouted that I was just getting some twigs for the fire and trampled in the bushes so she could hear me. I moved away but there was the snap of a lighter. The flare lit up his face briefly. His eyes were like chips of coal and his lashes looked an inch long. The light shone briefly on something round his ankle, which must have been the glint I had seen before.

"Who are you?" I said.

A thin stream of smoke came from his mouth. "The Wizard of the Forest," he said. The wizard was another character from the films I had done.

For a moment I didn't know whether I was acting or dreaming or what I was. I laughed. "There's no such thing as wizards and witches!"

The park bell rang. There was the snap of twigs. Mum called me again. "They're closing the gates, Des!"

"See me here on Halloween," he whispered. "And I'll prove it. It's our secret? Say nothing to your mum. If you do, you'll never see me again."

"Who - " I began but he vanished. He went so quick it was as if he had flown off. There was nothing but a faint cloud of blue smoke hanging where he was. And the smell of a cigarette. There were several footprints in the muddy grass. Crushed in one of them was a scrap of white. I picked up a bent cigarette end.

A light and something behind it crashed between two trees. It was mum. She shouted at me not to go off like that. Then she stopped. Sniffed.

"Was someone here? Someone smoking? Were you talking to someone?"

Her eyes were wild and staring and she grabbed me by the shoulders so much it hurt.

"Were you? Des? Was someone with you? Answer me!"

"There was a wizar -"

She shoved me away. "Stop clowning about will you! Don't go off in the dark like that! *Was* somone with you?"

I was really frightened of mum like that, even more than the wizard. I shook my head dumbly, and stumbled back with her through the trees to rejoin Em.

A wizard's arms were round me. They were squeezing me so tight I could scarcely breathe. There was a sharp snapping. Was it twigs or bones? It was my bones! Breaking. Used to make a fire, hot, so hot I was burning. Someone was screaming. The wizard was blocking my way.

"Des it's your mother ... your mum ... "

"He doesn't seem to recognise you," a tall figure who nearly reached the ceiling said. He seemed to be cut out of paper, with a permanent smile.

I was screaming and screaming and my pyjamas were all wet. My mum was holding me on one side of the bed, Almost on the other. At last I stopped struggling. She changed my pyjamas and stayed with me until at last I fell asleep again.

In the morning they kept trying to get me up. My eyes were tightly closed and I felt like I would never get up ever again. Eventually Mum pushed something under my nose. The smell of it woke me up all right. Through my flickering eyes I saw a cigarette end.

"Have you been smoking?"

"I found it."

"What made you pick up a disgusting thing like this?"

"Dunno."

"*Were* you smoking? Was it in those bushes -"

Almost put his hand on her arm. Her face was all twisted. I could see she had been crying. Her face was red and swollen. From Almost's watch it was only seven o'clock. I was still half-asleep. Why had mum been crying? All I had done was pick up a fag-end! I turned over again and shut my eyes.

"What on earth were you dreaming about?" Almost said.

"Didn't dream." I mumbled into the pillow. I didn't remember. Or didn't want to remember.

She touched me. "You had the most terrible dream darling! Don't you remem - "

"Didn't dream!" I shouted.

Almost led her away. "I'll take him to school," he said.

Several times I nearly fell asleep during class and only really woke up when we left school. It was Halloween. It was growing dark when parents came to collect us. Stewart's mum and others had Jack 'O Lanterns - cut-teethed pumpkins with candles.

Mandy said she would take me to a party in the park with Em, then go trick-or-treating. I was waiting for

Almost to collect me. I saw his peaked cap. Over his face he had a grinning, skull-shaped mask, holding out a barley sugar, shaped like a candle, with a big lick of cream on top, wrapped in a piece of paper with something scribbled on it.

My favourite! I unwrapped it and stuffed the paper in my pocket, sucking it lick by delicious lick. All the gloom and the nastiness of that morning was forgotten. I shouted to Em that Almost was here and turned back to tell him about the park party but couldn't see him. Most of the parents were moving off. Miss Hancock came over. I told her Almost had given me the barley-sugar which I had nearly finished.

"There he is! There's Almost." She pointed to his car, which he was getting out of. I ran over to him, thanking him for the barley sugar.

"What barley sugar?" he said.

I pointed to the end of the sweet clinging to my sticky fingers.

"You must thank someone else," he said. "I've only just got here. Sorry I was late."

I laughed. He was pretending! Worse than me! "Show me your mask."

"Mask?"

"Your skull mask! The one you were wearing under your peaked cap."

"My ..."

He looked up and down the street. His face was all twisted. "Get in the car," he said sharply.

"There's a party! Then we're trick-and-treating!"

Jess and Em were approaching. Em was grinning at me wearing a mask with jagged missing teeth.

"Sorry." he said. "You can't go."

"I said I'd go! "

"Your mum's very upset."

"I want to go! I'm with Mandy. I'll be ok."

I ran towards her.

"Des! Wait! Mandy!"

His voice rang down the street. He told me to wait with Em while he went a little distance away with Mandy. They huddled together, talking in low voices.

"What is it?" Em said.

"There's a ghost," I said.

"Don't be stupid!"

"Someone gave me this." I gave her a last suck at the barley sugar. "Can you see him?"

She jumped, glanced sharply up and down the street, then giggled. You are bonkers!"

"I'll prove it! I saw a person last evening in the park. He said he'd be there. Tonight. Don't tell my mum. Or Almost. Let's go. We'll be ok together. "

"Mum'll go spare ..."

"It's only round the corner! I'll look after you, Em."

"Will you, Des?

"I've always wanted a girl with rotten teeth. C'mon! Aren't you fed up of doing what you're told? Make a dash! We don't want to miss Halloween!"

I grabbed her and we ran. I could hear Almost running, shouting behind me. Em giggled. Stewart and the other kids cheered. Another street and we'd be in the park! One of her feet hit the kerb. Her mask fell off and she would have fallen if I hadn't caught her.

Almost grabbed me by the collar. I shouted and kicked at him. Who was Almost? He was a nobody. She would only get another feller. He gasped as I hit his knee. I nearly got away but he just caught my arm, twisted it behind me, marched me back to his car, forced me in, strapped me in the child-seat and began to drive off. I unstrapped myself and began to kick at the back of his seat. He parked again. I scrabbled out of the seat to unlock the door. There was a click. I pulled and pulled and pulled at the door catch. He had locked it.

I kicked and kicked at the back of his seat.

"Let me out! Let me out! Let me out! You're not my dad!"

"I know that, Des. I know that."

I went on kicking and shouting until I lost my breath and he just sat there and said nothing, nothing at all and now I *was* frightened. I wouldn't have been frightened of the man in the park, even if he was a ghost or a wizard but I was frightened of this man in front of me as he twisted round in his seat. His face *was* a mask. The black eyes didn't blink. His mouth was tight. The hair was starting to go in the middle. The big hands coming towards me were pitted with dirt and grease. I jerked away then, crying out that I wanted to go home. I wanted my mum!

He said very quiet, very still, and said "Let me fasten you in, then I will take you to your mum."

Click. Another click. I wasn't sure where he was taking me until I saw the yard by our flats and I ran up the stairs and there was mum at our open door and I didn't even believe it really was mum until I was in her arms and she was kissing me and hugging me and I was full of the smell of her.

She drew me away from her and said quietly. "Who is this man?"

"What man?"

"Who gave you the barley sugar?"

"Almost."

She shook her head. "The man with a mask ... *pretending* to be Almost ...?"

"I dunno. I just thought he was Almost."

"Did he try and take you in a car?"

"No! He just gave me a sweet, that's all!"

She said now I was working I musn't talk to strangers until I did get frightened and she became mum again. She fed me spag bol and my eyes began to close. I wanted her to put my pyjamas on and she laughed and said you put them on yourself now Des but she did it and I said "story" and she said you read one yourself now but she got me the one I wanted.

"Gingerbread Man?" she cried. "That was one of the very earliest you read yourself! When you were four or five!"

"Please!" I begged. "I just want that one now, that's all!"

I could smell him, the Gingerbread Man, as he was taken from the oven. I could hear him crying "You're not going to eat me!" I could hear him running from the little old woman, the pig and the cow and the horse. I clapped my hands as she read it. "Run run as fast as you can, you can't catch me - I'm the Gingerbread Man!"

But he couldn't cross the river. "I will help you," said the fox, and swam across the river with the Gingerbread Man on his back. As the fox climbed on the bank the Gingerbread Man saw the old woman, the pig, the cow and the horse.

"Ha ha," he said to the crowd across the river. "Now you can't eat me!" Then he asked the Fox how he could get down?

"Jump on my nose," said the Fox. So the Gingerbread Man did, but it was a trick -

A trick! Life was full of tricks! I dreamt of the Gingerbread Man sliding towards the Fox's wide open mouth. There was a gulp and I woke up. It was the bang of the closing door. I heard Almost talking to mum.

"Do you want me out?"

"Out? What on earth are you talking about?"

"Until this business is settled."

"Don't be stupid! That's the last thing I want! "

Their voices dropped to a murmur. I crept out of my room towards the door .

"Do you think it was him?" Mum said. "Did you see him without his mask?"

"Didn't see him at all. But Des told me he had a light round his ankle. Which he thought was part of the wizard flying."

"What do you think it was?"

"A curfew tag they put on you when you're being released."

A curfew tag? Being released? Was he being released from prison? Is that what they meant? There was the clink of glasses and the sound of something being poured and a long silence then, just as I moved again to open the door Almost spoke.

"Tell him who you think it is."

He was so near the door at which I was listening I jumped, knocking something over. I heard her cry out and ran for my bed. It was half-game and half-fear of them being so angry at me listening, well spying, that's what it was, wasn't it? Spying. I have never got into bed more fast. It was odd. All this pretend - be this person, be that, that Zoe and the others were making me do as Wes, Wild Boy, was beginning to work. As soon as I shot back into bed I was still. Quite still. I shut my eyes. It was as if I was being photographed. Filmed. I felt as if I was on the edge of sleep as I heard Mum come into my room.

"Ssshh!" she whispered. "He's well away. It must have been someone on the stairs."

She began to tuck me in. At the murmur of their voices I couldn't stand the pretend any longer and began to feel a smile building up. At any moment laughter would burst out.

"Look at him!" Mum said. "I wonder what he's dreaming about."

"Don't wake him!" Almost hissed. "Not now! For God's sake!"

He pulled her away. I daren't leave the bed again but I didn't have to. They left the door open and I caught enough of their voices as they drank some more and his voice got louder.

"Does he know his dad is on limited access from prison?"

"No."

Through the gap in the half-open door I could see Almost pacing about. "You know why his father's interested in him now, don't you?"

"Because my little boy is a star," she said, in a voice half-sad, but I thought, half-proud.

A star? Is that what I was? Des a star? But even more than that I had a Dad like other boys had. A Dad who wanted to see me! He was the man in the mask, the man in the park! Why was she stopping me from seeing him? Who was he? What had he done? I jumped out of bed. I wanted to see my dad!

When I reached the door I saw Mum had her face in her hands and Almost had his arms round her. "I know, she said. "I know. I'll have to tell him. I've been stupid. I thought his dad would just forget me and I was determined to forget about him and, and, when Des was a bit older he'd be in a better position to understand ..."

I went into the room. I could understand now, I was sure. But they were in the middle of a kiss. I stopped, upset, confused. Somehow I didn't like her kissing Almost now I knew I had a Dad.

She pulled away from him. Their eyes were so much on each other they never turned, never saw me. "But he won't see his Dad," she said. "Not until he's old enough to understand."

"Can you stop him from seeing Des?"

"Of course I can stop him. And I will go on stopping him for as long as I possibly can!"

Oh no you won't, I whispered to myself, as I crept back into my bed. Oh no you won't. Not now I'm a star. And I have a dad. Like other people. You can't stop me from seeing my dad. You can't stop a star from doing what he wants to do.

Kerfew

I was the wurst speller in the klass (sumbody else has korected most of this, haven't u guessed?) So Miss Hancock was surprised when I asked how to spell *K -e- r - f - e - w*.

"Well, I think you mean *c - u - r - f-e-w*. It's an order, saying you have to be in a certain place at a certain time. Like when you have to be in school at a certain time."

"And what's a tag? T-a-g?"

"Do you mean label, Des?"

I didn't know. But labels, labels ... On Almost's computer at home I found "electronic tagging." It included ankle monitors used during the time when people were being released from prison. *That* was what glinted on his ankle when I saw him in the park!

My Dad was being *let out* of prison! He was a *real* Wild Boy! He wanted to see his son - his son! - and I wanted to see him! Just because he'd done something wrong *why* couldn't I see him? I'd done plenty of wrong things! We could share wrong things together!

"Food's ready!" Mum shouted.

I rushed into the kitchen. "Is my Da-"

"Sit down!" she said. Then: "Hands!" As soon as I showed her them she said. "Bathroom. Now."

I dipped my hands under the tap, wiped them and rushed back then saw what was on my plate. Burger and chips. Stars whose dads were leaving prison didn't eat burgers. They ate sausages. Best chipolatas. I shoved my plate away, spilling some of the chips on the table and the floor.

"Suit yourself," she said. "If you don't eat, you don't eat."

I folded my arms and stuck my lips out. She had put tomato sauce on the table when she *knew* I hated tomato and ate HP!

She poured herself a glass of wine. Her hand shook and some spilled on the cloth. It was from the bottle she had been drinking with Almost the night before. She took a swallow then poured more in.

"Desmond ... The man you saw in the park ... the man who gave you that barley sugar -"

"My dad?" I said.

Her mouth dropped open, bigger than I'd ever seen it. Nearly as big as her face. Wine slopped all over from her glass as she put it down.

"The man in prison?"

"Oh Des ... Des! I'm sorry, I'm so sorry ... You *did* hear last night ... I wondered ... I should have told you ... I don't know what I should have done ..." Her drink was on the floor with my burger and chips and I was in her arms and I was half-crying, half-laughing because the nastiness had gone and she was mum again, hugging and holding and kissing me. I could smell the food.

"Can I have a chip?"

"You can have as many chips as you like, darling ... as many chips as ...Oh Des ... oh Des ... you are ... I don't know what you are ... I don't know who you are half the time ..." She was laughing and crying and we ate chips together until we had finished every single chip on the plate.

"Can I see him?"

"No. No ... He's ... he's in prison."

"I saw him in the park.."

"He wasn't supposed to be. He's allowed out. Not everywhere. Not near you." There was a little bit of wine left in the glass she had knocked over. She finished it, put her hands on my shoulders and said: "Listen Des ... He can't see you ... and you can't see him."

"Why?"

"Because he's done some nasty things. That's why he's in prison."

"What things?"

"Drugs. Deals in them and takes them. She gripped my shoulder so tightly it hurt. "Has he given you anything?"

"No. No. Only that barley sugar."

"I wouldn't have trusted that ... "

"Barley sugar?"

"If it was barley sugar ... I don't know what to say ..." She poured herself more wine.

I watched her have one swallow. Then another. "Aren't you drinking too much, mum?"

She stared at me, her mouth dropping open again, then put the glass down and burst out laughing. We were in the kitchen, and she poured the rest of the glass in the sink.

She was shaking. She didn't seem to be able to stop shaking. She walked one way, then another, as if she didn't know where she was then she said: "Yes Des, you're right, you're absolutely right, I am... drinking far too much ... I am ..." She hugged me and kissed the top of my head. "Perhaps you should be the one looking after me." She wiped the back of her hand over her eyes.

"Perhaps my dad's better," I said.

"Better? What do you mean ... better?"

"Miss Hancock told me people go to prison to be punished and to learn to be better."

She picked up her glass again and put it down and gripped my shoulders again so tight it hurt. "Listen Des ... you are not to go anywhere near your father. Not now. Not until you're older. He is *not* to be trusted. Do you understand?"

She bent over me, speaking so fiercely there was nothing I could do but nod. It made me afraid of dad. For a bit. But it also made me more curious. More wanting to see him. Have a dad like other children. What was there not to be trusted? I kept looking for his face at collection time and in the park. But there was no sign of him and at first, the way mum and Almost guarded me, I felt as if *I* was in a kind of prison

"What has he done?" Em asked.

"Drugs."

"Oh." She shrugged. "Lots of mum's friends do drugs. I see them at shoots."

That was right. When the set was being laid the cameraman always smoked and smelt of a wood fire.

Every day I expected the wizard to appear but nothing happened. Nothing. It got dark earlier. The park shut early. They stopped guarding me so much. I stopped looking out for him. He was like a ghost who had vanished. Then one day the weather changed. It looked as if it would always be summer but it was really cold. Mum brought out my winter jacket and wanted to take the summer one to the cleaners. She chucked it to me.

"The pockets are full of rubbish. You clear it out."

Among the sweet wrappings and my cycle keys were scraps of paper with phone numbers and pictures of football players. At the bottom of one pocket my fingers felt a mess of sticky goo. I pulled out my hand and untangled the scrap of paper which had been wrapped round the barley sugar my ghost had given me - funnily enough, I had stopped thinking of him as my dad, but my ghost.

I shoved it among the other rubbish and was about to drop it in the bin when I saw part of a line scribbled on it: *email your* ... I threw the rest in and unpicked the barley sugar paper. The message finished: ... *dad at Wildman31.co.uk.*

"Do you want me to put that in the wash or not?"

I looked up to see my mum, her face half-hidden by the clothes she was holding. I could feel the tightness of her grip on my shoulders and hear her voice again warning me not to go anywhere near my father. She must be able to see the scrap of paper in my hand. I should give it to her. I should give -

"Des!"

I just gave her the jacket.

For the first time for ages I wasn't being picked up by Mum or Almost. Mandy was collecting me from school with Em. Mandy said she would buy some sausages because she had done a vegetarian meal which she knew I hated. To her surprise and Em's I said I would like to try it.

It was crap but I smuggled half back into the container it had come from and forced down the rest.

"If she'd got sausages I'd never have done it before Mum got here." I mumbled.

"Done what?" Em said.

We scrambled into the television room and Em switched on Horrid Henry. But for once we didn't watch him trying to escape from Miss Battle-Axe. Em had an old computer. While I tried to get it to work she stared at the scribble on the barley-sugar paper.

"You're not going to e-mail your dad?"

"Why not?

The computer creaked and groaned and a coloured wheel whirled round in the middle of it, then vanished and asked me for my passcode.

I looked at Em. She bit her lip. Her teeth looked very white. "I don't think you should do this."

"He is my dad." I was calling him dad again. "And the prison people will see it."

She gave me the code.: "Two-zero-one-zero."

Dear Dad, I wrote. Sorry never answered this till now but I only saw yr email when I emptied my pockets.

Mandy came in. She was behind my back and if she looked down she would see my e-mail, but she looked at the screen where Henry was being tweaked up by the ear.

"What's it like being vegan, Des?"

I could not think of what to say. I felt she must be staring at the screen but if I pulled it down it would draw her attention to it. Then I remembered what my mum had said when she had some food at somebody's house and hated it.

"Interesting."

She burst out laughing and squeezed my shoulder. "I know where you got that from." She pointed to the window. My mum was smiling and waving. "I was at the same dinner. "

My whole mind went blank. My finger went to delete what I had done but I heard them talking and laughing in the hall and wrote all frantic: r u going to be out soon? Des. Yr son. PS thank u for the barley sugar.

Dear Son:

Great to hear from you. I am so proud of you. When I saw your picture in the papers I could not stop looking at it. It is on the wall of my cell. The first thing I see when I wake up in the morning, and the last thing when they turn out the lights at night.

Yes. I am going to be out soon. When they let me out for a bit and I saw you she told the police I came to your school which I was not supposed to and they banged me up again. I will get into trouble if they know I am writing to you. DO NOT SHOW HER THIS EMAIL OR ANYONE. It is a secret e-mail prisoners use.

Keep writing son.

Yr Dad. x

Son, he wrote. Son. He was my Dad! He was in prison again for trying to see me! Mum told them! *She* had him put in prison again! *She* was preventing me from seeing my Dad! At first, time after time, I went up to her to ask her *why? Why can't I see him?* But each time I saw the look on her face I remembered what he had written: YOU MUST NOT SHOW HER THIS.

I knew, once I began talking about it everything would come out. They might lock him up even longer.

Several times she said "What is it Des?" and I found some excuse, waiting for the time when I was next going to Em's and got his message. Once or twice I couldn't bear waiting and I sneaked and used Almost's computer again.

I discovered I had a different name. I was Des Taylor. I had been born Desmond Walker. My Dad was Mike Walker. He seemed almost as daft as me. Dad knew I watched Horrid Henry and he called Mum Mrs Battle-Axe. I didn't know whether to laugh at that or not. He sent a picture of himself looking out of a window in a prison door, sticking his tongue out. Then he said we must stop. He was going to be out of prison after Christmas and had to behave himself. He would try and see me when he was out.

Out

On Christmas day among the presents was a Funny Football book and a big card saying *Merry Christmas YOUR DAD*.

One-two-three - FOUR places laid at the table for Christmas dinner! FOUR Christmas crackers. "Is he coming?" I said, doing my excited flap-a-hands. The outside door was opening and Almost was letting someone in.

"No darling," she said, giving Almost a look as he pulled the door wide-open and let Grandad in.

"So far as we know," Almost said.

He didn't come that day or the next. I asked her when he was coming and we had one of those long sit-down discussions in which she said when someone left prison it was difficult. He had to sort himself out.

"Have you seen him?" she said, sudden and sharp.

"No! I want to see him!"

"I know, I know love!" she said, holding me tightly. "I know you do but -" She couldn't keep still. She jumped up, locked the door and then went back to check if she had locked it.

When I was with Em at her house I tried the prison e-mail I had used before but it said: *No connection*. Once, when Almost picked me up from school, and we were going upstairs to the flat I heard loud bursts of her voice on the phone.

"No Mike no!"

Mike. My Dad. She began to shout on the phone.

"*I will not Mike!* ... no no no, I've told you, you'll have to wait until the court hearing, until the judge -"

Almost did a loud rat-a-tat-tat on the door before we went in. Her voice sank down to a mumble and when we went in there was no sign of the phone and there was a smile on her face to greet me.

Court? Judge? I didn't know what it all meant, what was going on. I used to have my supper on the kitchen table while they talked about my day. Now they dumped me in front of the telly to eat while they talked together. At first having meals watching the telly was ok. Then I got fed up. Every time I went into the kitchen they stopped talking.

One day, when Almost was working late at the garage, Mum gave me supper in the kitchen and it was just like it used to be. Homework. I had written a story for Miss Hancock about a robber who was in prison.

"His name is Mike and he was told he would be let out of prison if he promised to rob no more so he promised. Clang went the gates. It was lovely outside at first. He saw his son and took him to football. Then his money ran out and he had no job. He thought well, at least they give you something to eat in prison so he went to some houses where rich people live. He was looking for a house to rob when he saw a woman with a lot of shopping, trying to open a gate which was stuck so much that she dropped something. It was a handbag full of money. Well, he thought, that's not robbery. I found it. But he remembered his promise and he gave her the handbag and fixed her gate and she was rich and paid him and he did other work for her and stayed out of prison and watched his son score lots and lots of goals. THE END.

Mum coughed and cleared her throat and said: "That's very nice, Des, but, but -"

"But what? Doesn't it have a Dilemma, a Climax and a Conclusion?"

I looked at her. She wiped her eyes and her voice sounded all funny and she said: "It certainly has a Dilemma, Des, but er ..."

The flat bell rang. I ran to the door. I could just reach the door latch on the tip of my toes. Looking down at me, his helmet in his hands, was a policeman.

"My Dad's not here," I said.

"Why it's PC Desmond!"

I realised it was Sergeant Wilcox. I was starting to mumble that I wasn't a policeman no more when Mum pushed me to one side and told me to put my pyjamas on. I went to my bedroom and scrambled fast into them so I could creep back to the kitchen door. The policeman had put his helmet on the kitchen table and was taking out a note-book.

"It's Mr Fraser I want," he said. "AKA Almost?"

I crept back back towards the kitchen. Mr Fraser? *Almost*? "We would like to question him about ... erm an incident ... and erm Mike Walker has, er ..."

Mike Walker? My dad? I reached the kitchen door.

"Mr Walker has expressed concern about the safety of his son ..."

Mum's mouth dropped open. Her eyes were as big as saucers. "Safety? Mike Walker has expressed concerns about the safety of his son? From - from Almost - I mean from Mr *Fraser*?"

"Yes madam."

She laughed, opened her mouth, was unable to speak then shook her head. "You're joking. You - are - joking!"

Sergeant Wilcox coughed and cleared his throat again. He looked again at the papers. "Mr Walker is Desmond Walker's father?"

Mum gripped the table. She looked as if she was holding on to it. She stared at our empty plates. At my school bag with the story about my Dad poking out. "Yes," she choked. "Yes."

"We have to investigate these matters."

She turned away. She saw me. "Go- to-bed-Desmond!"

I ran, half-knocking a chair over. I didn't know what I was doing or where I was going. Or who I was. I blundered into things until I pulled the mattress and pillows over me.

It was the day at school I liked best. When we were out of school in the afternoon playing football in the park. Stewart was captain of the Red side and Mr Hunter made me captain of the Blue side. He had the whistle in his mouth ready to blow it when we were winning three-two. Most of our side was in their goal area and I ran to join in but the ball sailed out to Stewart their striker. I ran. He was going to shoot. I had never slid faster. Stewart missed and fell.

Mr Hunter blew his whistle. "Good tackle Des! Well played everyone - very close!"

I grinned at him. Other players were all round me, slapping me on the back. I felt better than I had been for ages. Stewart picked himself up, covered in mud. When we were changing he came up to me.

"Your second dad is going to prison," he said. "Like your first."

It was the look on his face. Everything that had happened. I don't know what it was. I went for him and hit him and hit him until Mr Hunter pulled me off him. I don't remember what they said to me. My head was ringing and I couldn't hear them. In the school they now had an isolation booth. They dragged me in there. I tried to tell them what Stewart had said but they wouldn't listen and locked me in there until Mum collected me. It was a prison. I was in prison like my father. I shouted and shouted until I had no voice left.

She marched me all the way home. She said she had warned me never, ever, ever again to have a go at Stewart. The son of Almost's employer? I started to tell her it was *him*! What he said to me - but she wouldn't listen. She kept talking all the way up the stairs to our flat until she saw the door open and stopped. There were sounds inside. Almost was packing a haversack.

"What are you doing?" she said.

"Going."

"Where?"

He shrugged.

"Prison?" I said.

"That's what your dad would like to see," Almost said. He began fastening the haversack. "Is that what you want as well?"

"Come on come on come on!" Mum cried. "Des doesn't *know* what's going on!"

"Doesn't he? Oh doesn't he?" He got out his computer and brought up a message I'd sent to my dad which I thought I'd deleted. "That kid always knows much more than you bloody well think." He chucked the computer back in his haversack. "Don't you?"

Mum sat down on the bed, closed her eyes and dropped her face in her hands. Almost slung his haversack on and reached the door before Mum sat up.

"Have the police been questioning you?"

Almost stopped by the door. He spoke to the door more than to Mum that my dad was pulling him into it again. He said it was when he repaired cars for Mr Magic, before he realised he was a robber, but Mum stopped him and told me to go to bed.

He turned on me like he used to. I thought for a minute he was going to go for me. Mum pulled me to her then told me again to go to bed.

"He should hear this," Almost said. "He's grown-up now. Or likes to think he is."

Mum glared at me, swallowed, then told me all sharp to sit down. Not to interrupt.

"Yes, mum," I said quietly. I had to bite my lips to stop myself from smiling at the look on their faces. Grown-up now! I didn't have to creep around listening, trying to understand what was going on. When Almost said he hadn't been sacked from the garage but suspended I asked what sus-pen-ded meant.

"For - the - moment," Mum said. "Then why are you going?" she said to Almost.

"He wants his dad here, don't you?"

"Oh don't be stupid!" Mum cried. "I certainly don't! He wants to *see* his dad ..." She got up and went close to him. They seemed to forget I was there. She touched his face, then the haversack. "Take that off. Come on."

He gripped her arm, then looked at me and moved sharply away.

"You want your dad, don't you?" He walked about the room touching things, staring out of the window, before coming back to me. "Don't you? Don't you?"

"Yes." I said.

I suddenly didn't know what I wanted. I thought I understood everything but now I felt I understood nothing nothing nothing.

"You sent him all those letters," Almost said.

"What letters!" Mum cried.

"I told you! He's been using my computer. I'll bet you've been using others haven't you?"

It came out. All of it. Now all I wanted was to go to my own room and hide. If this was what being a grown-up was like I never wanted to grow up anymore. I wanted to go back to where I was.

Now everybody was talking and nobody was listening and Almost was slinging his rucksack over his shoulder again. We collided as we tried to leave the room together and I fell and as Almost picked me up we saw that Mum had sat down, arms folded with that look on her face.

She shook her head very slow. "Go on then, both of you. Go on go on. You to your Dad, you to wherever, Almost."

She looked as if she meant it. I couldn't stop crying as I ran to her, and she put her arms round me, tears coming.

"Come here ... come here you little idiot ... I didn't mean it ... of course I didn't mean it but ... sometimes ... sometimes ... you you ..."

I held on to my mum. "I don't want to grow up no more."

She laughed. "Don't you love? I wish I wasn't sometimes. Men. Men." She looked at me, then at Almost, who never stopped playing with his haversack.

"You want me to stay, then?"

"Well I certainly don't want to face him on my own," she snapped.

It was Saturday. I woke up early and couldn't get back to sleep. I was going to go out with dad. It had taken ages. There were strange people called law-yers and arguments between mum and dad but now I was going to go out with him for the afternoon. He was coming for me at two o'clock. My new dad! I kept looking out for him appearing in the yard. Mum walked about the flat. She kept coming up behind me. I'd only ever met him in the dark and didn't know what to look out for.

The bell rang. I stayed where I was. So did mum. It rang again. Longer. I went out into the hall. Mum grabbed me, then opened the door.

He was thin and as pale as the ghost in the park and had a smile which kept coming and going. He had on the kind of boiler suit which Almost wore.

"Jess." he said to Mum, with a sharp nod.

She had no smile at all. None. "Mike." A sharp nod.

I crept round mum's jeans. I couldn't look at him or know what to say to him at first.

"Where are you taking him?"

He shook his head. "Dunno. Where's he taking me?"

It was funny. He said I was taking him out. He said he'd been Inside. I had to show him Outside. I knew Outside and he'd forgotten what it was like. He was always joking, playing games and kept me laughing, but somehow I couldn't call him dad. He said where did I want to go?

"The zoo," I said.

"You can't go there Des - it's too much!" she said.

Somehow he was different, standing stiff and still, his smiles all gone. "It's my afternoon, Jess."

Then the smiles came back and he was joking again, saying he had been saving up for this, and he could understand why a Wild Boy wanted to see the zoo - Wild Life. While she was buttoning my coat she whispered to me not to ask him for too many things. He took me there in an old van in which he delivered stuff for a building firm.

We went into the monkey house. I made faces at the monkeys through the glass and they stuck their tongues out at me. Then he turned his bottom towards the glass and they turned their bums at him. We hopped out of the monkey house together unable to say anything because we were laughing so much. We then went into a shop which was full of monkey puzzles, videos and T-shirts.

One of the Skywalker T-shirts was terrific. On the chest was a monkey parting the branches of a tree sticking out its tongue. We laughed at it and made faces at it.

"Would you like it?"

I looked up at him, still laughing and was about to say "yes please dad" when I remembered mum telling me not to ask for things and shook my head and turned to go out of the shop. When I got to the door he wasn't there. I couldn't see him. It was like those first times I had seen him in the park and then at school, seen him and then he'd suddenly vanished.

I went back inside the shop and he appeared from the shopping queue holding a bag with the monkey shirt in it. I just stood there. I wanted it but I didn't know what mum would say. He held it out to me.

"Do you want it or not?" he said.

I took it and he told me to put it on and I did. "Thank you." I swallowed. I had been looking forward all this time to seeing him and I realised I had never used the word. "Thank you, dad."

He slapped me on the back and we grunted like monkeys again while we ate pizzas and I had so much ice-cream I fell asleep in the van. I didn't know where I was and who was shaking me for a moment. He put his phone to my ear and my mum's voice was shouting where was I? What was I doing?

He made paw scratches under his elbows and I laughed and grunted.

"What?" she shouted. "Are you all right?"

"Yes mum. I'm a monkey."

He took back the phone and I could hear her being angry while he said he was sorry, but he had had to collect some bricks on a job he was on. I saw someone dumping a cardboard box as I fell asleep again. The next time I woke up the van was in the yard outside the flats and mum was waiting. She stared at my T-shirt.

"I've been to the zoo, mum!"

"Have you darling."

She turned to him and gave him a smile that wasn't a smile and as I walked away I couldn't stop talking to her about the zoo, looking back as the van bumped out of the yard and he gave a monkey wave to me and I gave one back. I had a dad. A real dad.

Mum had got pizza for me that night which I couldn't eat - I was full of pizza. I couldn't stop talking about the zoo. She nodded and smiled but I could see she was somewhere else.

She was on duty that night at the hospital and while she changed into her nurse's uniform I asked her why she had left dad. She was buttoning her coat and put buttons in the wrong holes and had to do them up all over again. She turned away, wiped the back of her hand over her eyes, and said: "Why don't you ask him that?"

Almost put me to bed. He didn't seem interested in the zoo. He asked me where we went afterwards. I said I didn't know. I was asleep.

"Did he collect something?" Almost said.

I remembered what he said to mum on the phone and told him he picked up some bricks from somewhere.

"Bricks?" he said, with a smile.

There was something in the way he smiled I didn't like. I told him I would read my own story. He couldn't read proper anyway. He shrugged and went off. He suddenly wasn't Almost. Perhaps he was Never. I didn't know who he was.

Next day at school I wore my monkey T-shirt and Miss Hancock said how nice it was.

"My dad bought it," I said.

"Almost," she said.

"No. My dad. My *proper* dad," I said.

He *was* a proper dad. Like Stewart's dad. The hospital wanted Mum to work longer, and because Almost was suspended she had to. He hadn't a car for the school runs and dad started doing them. Almost was out a lot and started arguing with mum. Once he was away for a couple of days and came back late at night. I thought he was gone for good. Then one night their loud voices woke me.

"If you want things to change get a job!" Mum said.

"There's only one way I can do that," Almost said.

"Go on.

"Prove what Des's dad's up to."

I crept out. It was like going into a story, a dream, like happened before.

"I can't! He's his Dad! You know what Des feels about him!"

"Keep your voice down!"

This time she caught me. I was still half-asleep. "What he's up to, Mum?" I mumbled.

"What?"

"Dad... All he's up to is collecting me from school and building things ...."

"Yes ... yes, I know darling. Go back to sleep."

One Thursday dad came to see me playing football in the park.

"Why do you never score?" he said.

"Because I'm a *defender* dad," I said. "I stop goals." I told him Mr Hunter said defenders were just as important.

"Even defenders score," he said. "And their goals are even better - because they're unexpected."

He said that on a day when he had a cold - he was sniffing, so I determined to make him feel better. The other school was winning by a goal. I got the ball, heard Mr Taylor shout to me to pass to Stewart who could get an easy goal but their goalie was out of position and I sent in a long curving shot over his head. I scored!

I was so excited I ran over to where dad was standing. He wasn't there! He wasn't watching! I ran to the railings, through which I could see the road where he was parked. He chucked aside my jacket which I had left there. He was pulling up my car seat. With him was a big man, someone I thought I had seen before. Beneath the car seat was a compartment from which he took a large box. Small packets fell from it. On them was red flashes of forked lightning. The big man smiled at me and seemed to make the packets vanish. It was Mr Magic!

I shouted at my Dad. He looked up as Mr Hunter yelled at me from the pitch to get back in position. The kick-off had started. I was so far out of position the other side scored. My dad saw that. And Mr Hunter shaking his head at me. I was gutted.

"Great goal, Des," Stewart said, with a smile but a nasty look.

I turned on him. I didn't go for him this time. But I told him to fuck off. Mr Hunter took me to one side and said he had been through all this before and I would miss the next game. Everything was spinning round me. Nothing else mattered to me at that moment more than football.

Dad was whistling as he took me to his car. "Well done," he said. "Great game."

I wonder if he saw anything. I wonder if he cared. He didn't feel like my dad then. Didn't look like him. There something really funny about him. His eyes looked very large. He kept whistling. The car was like it was. My jacket was exactly where I had left it.

"What were you doing?" I said.

"Doing?" His eyes looked even larger.

"With - was it Mr Magic?"

He grabbed me by my arms. His face was twisted and his breath smelled funny and he was more eyes than face. He wasn't my dad, I don't know who he was. "You saw nothing! You were playing football. Weren't you? Weren't you?"

I couldn't speak. I nodded and kept nodding.

He dumped me in the car. My car seat was exactly where it was. He clicked the belt in. Slowly his face changed and his smile returned. "That's the spirit. That's the boy."

He winked. I managed to wink back.

In your own words

I ran up the stairs to the flats when dad left me and hammered at our door. I never knew who would be there these days, Mum or Almost. No-one answered. I kicked at it.

"All right, all right, steady on!"

It was Grandad. I felt even more low. He took forever and ever to open the door. Almost's jacket was hanging on my hook. I chucked mine on top of it. They both fell off. I didn't care. I just flung myself on my bed. He poked me with his stick. I knocked it away.

"Hey hey hey," he said. "Didn't you have a good game?"

" We lost," I muttered.

"We all have to lose sometime," he said.

"I don't."

He laughed and went to put a packet of food on. I said I wasn't hungry.

There was a pain in my stomach where dad had grabbed me and shoved me in the car. But it was spag bol and once I started I shoved it down and then I suddenly felt sick and it all came up over Grandad. He cleaned me up and got me back to bed.

Mum phoned up and I wanted her so much but she was working and there was no sign of Almost and I didn't know if I wanted him or what. Then at last

I began to feel sleepy but Grandad shuffled in and sat slowly on the end of the bed. He stared across at me. He was somehow a different kind of Grandad, with a different kind of voice. He dumped down my jacket I had worn to football, together with Almost's jacket, in front of me. Caught between them was a small packet. On it was a red flash of forked lightning.

"Where did this come from, Des?" he said, his voice very quiet.

I remembered Mr Magic. The seat in my dad's car pulled up and the compartment behind it, the packets spilling from the box, with bits of forked lightning. My eyes were still half-closed. Was it all part of a dream? Then I woke sharply. Fear grabbed me as I saw again my dad's face. All eyes. His voice: "You saw nothing! You were playing football. Weren't you? Weren't you?"

I shook my head. "Dunno. I dunno."

Grandad now showed me the jacket he had picked up with mine. "Whose is this?"

"Almost's."

Grandad turned out my light and once again I began to drift into sleep. But I heard Grandad on the phone.

"... Gerald Foot ... used to be Inspector Foot of the Shepherds Road branch..."

That woke me up. I sat up. "I've found a packet of the drugs you're looking for ... I'm looking after my grandson ... That's right, his dad is Mike Walker, just released from prison -"

There was a long silence. I felt they were going to arrest my Dad. I jumped out of bed, I don't know what I was going to say but I heard Grandad laughing.

Laughing! I stopped at the door.

"Mike Walker behaving himself is he? ..."

Dad?

"... I'm glad to hear it. In fact, I believe the drugs dropped from the jacket of Stephen Nesbitt..."

Almost? Not dad? I shut my eyes with relief and staggered slowly back to bed with my eyes more than half-way closed. Even when he stuck his head round the door I never opened them.

In the morning they seemed glued together even when Mum pulled me out of bed and threw my clothes at me at the same time as she was giving Grandad breakfast. Almost had been arrested.

Grandad cut a large piece of bacon and chewed it with a piece of egg, yellow trickling down to his chin. "They can't do without me," he said.

"Are you sure the packet was in Almost's jacket?" she said.

"Dropped from it." He chewed. "I did tell you ... drove cars for a previous drug run. Tried to claim he didn't know what it was." He sniffed, shook his head, chewed. "I did er ... warn you when you first went out with him..."

She was cutting another bacon sandwich and I thought she was going to throw it or the knife at him but she turned away and shoved the sandwich at me. I was still half-asleep and eating the end of the sandwich as she hurried me along to school. She told me my dad was picking me up.

I swallowed the last of the sandwich and shook my head all violent.

"What's that mean?" Mum said.

"No," I said.

"No what?"

"No thank you."

She stopped suddenly, jerking me so I nearly fell. I felt sick again.

"I mean you love your Dad, you *want* him to pick you up don't you? Des? Don't you?"

I was sick. The whole of the sandwich and I don't know what else came up. She grabbed me and held me over the gutter. She took me into a Costa, got herself a coffee and me a water, phoned the hospital, said she would be in late and the school to tell them I wouldn't be in at all.

"All right," she said, doing her folded-arms look. "Tell me."

I told her. Everything. Her mouth dropped open and stayed open until I finished and she said: "Is this true? Or one of your stories?"

I burst into tears. She didn't believe me! She would never believe me! I had lost my mum forever and would be lost in one of my stories forever! I got up, knocking her coffee over and was going to run out but she grabbed me and held me and said she believed me, it was all right she believed me, she knew what my dad was like. He was such a good schemer even she had been beginning to believe what he had told her - that he was beginning to be the good dad, a real father! But he had been using it as a perfect cover to sell drugs to people inside the prison he'd been in.

She was mum. Mum was back. Everything will be all right now, she said. Now you've told me. You've done the right thing.

The tears were coming again. "What about Grandad?"

"What about him?"

"He's arrested Almost. And he's an *Inspector!*"

"Grandad ... Yes. Well ..." She coughed and swallowed the remains of her coffee.

"Erm ... even Grandad made mistakes in his later years." She pulled on my jacket. She spoke more to herself than me. "I think that's why they promoted him."

She took me to the police station. I was very frightened at first. I thought they were going to arrest me but gradually I got bored. Very bored. There was no handcuffs and no guns. It was all about cars wrongly parked and motor-cyclists on pavements and drinking. It was hot and smelly. At last we were shown into a room. There was Sergeant Wicklow, who had come to our flat.

"Hello, young man," he said. "You again. You've become a PC again, have you?

He switched some recording thing on and told me to tell him what happened when my dad took me to football.

"Tell it in your own words," he said.

"I wouldn't do that if I were you," Mum muttered.

"What?" said Sergeant Wicklow, switching off. "I'm sorry?"

Mum put her head in her hands. I think she was crying. I put my hand on hers now.

"I'm sorry, I'm sorry," she said, "but I think I've lost my job now. We've all lost our jobs".

"Have I lost my school?" I said.

For the first time, for a long time, there might have been a smile on Mum's face. "No darling," she said. "I'm afraid not."

There certainly was a smile on Sergeant Wicklow's face now. "Family affair, is it?" he said.

"You can put it like that," Mum said. "No story Des," Mum said. "No story. Just tell Sergeant Wilcox what happened."

Miss Hancock read what I had written: "Famlee affair, is it? the Sarjant said."
THE END.

She closed my English paper and smiled. "I think that's easily the best story you've ever written, Des, but do watch your spelling!"

Almost had collected me from school for the first time since Sergeant Wicklow had arrested him, and he had had to go back to the garage to finish repairing a car. We hadn't talked much. I think he blamed me for siding with my Dad. I never knew what Almost thought. Early that morning Dad had been caught by the police trying to leave the country in his new big car. I hadn't slept proper since he was on the run but I felt I would tonight.

Almost was underneath a car in the shed, fixing a broken exhaust.

"I got A plus for my story which wasn't really a story, " I said.

Almost grunted and his hand came out from under the car scrabbling for a spanner he had put down. I passed it to him. He grunted. I liked Almost's hands. They were always dirty. Always moving. A screw dropped and rolled. I caught it and gave it to him.

He grunted. Coughed. Screwed. "Sorry about your dad," he mumbled.

"I'm not."

He threw out the old, rusted exhaust. I chucked it in the metal rubbish bin and said: "He's not my dad. You are."

He crawled out from under the car and heaved himself up. "No I'm not," he grunted.

My heart sank into my boots. I thought he still blamed me for his arrest. But then he raised his dirty hand. "I'm Almost."

I lifted my hand which was now Almost as dirty as his and we slapped hands together.

"Almost," I said.

"C'mon," he said. "Let's go home."

Lightning Source UK Ltd.
Milton Keynes UK
UKHW012242200721
387486UK00002BA/113

9 781839 751523